DEAD MAN UPRIGHT

Derek Raymond

Little, Brown and Company

A *Little, Brown* Book

First published in Great Britain in 1993
by Little, Brown and Company

Copyright © Derek Raymond 1993

The moral right of the author has been asserted.

*All characters in this publication are fictitious and
any resemblance to real persons, living or dead,
is purely coincidental.*

All rights reserved.
No part of this publication may be reproduced,
stored in a retrieval system, or transmitted, in any
form or by any means, without the prior
permission in writing of the publisher, nor be
otherwise circulated in any form of binding or
cover other than that in which it is published and
without a similar condition including this
condition being imposed on the subsequent purchaser.

A CIP catalogue record for this book is
available from the British Library.

ISBN 0 316 90682 4

Typeset in Plantin by Solidus (Bristol) Limited
Printed and bound in Great Britain by
Clays Ltd, St Ives plc

Little, Brown and Company (UK) Limited
165 Great Dover Street
London SE1 4YA

For Marie

Tous les criminels sont des jésuites...

1

Jidney put a finger in his ear and withdrew some wax.

'Sixteen,' he murmured, studying it, 'that's one every one point two two years recurring.' There was a need to accelerate. He shut his eyes and the face of his new love, Ann, appeared. 'For sixteen you can say seventeen soon,' he whispered. He gazed into the sitting-room mirror; he was a man exalted, in a hurry.

Flora's tin might as well join the others this evening. He found it in the trousers he had worn last night; it had once contained acid drops. He opened it, put his lips to the contents and touched them for a while; then he sealed the tin with tape, smiling and talking to himself. He marked the spot on the carpet with his heel where it had to go; then, turning back into the bedroom, straightened his tie yet again in an effort to maintain his good humour. After doing what was necessary in the country and driving back to London he had gone to bed, slept soundly and woken in a state of tranquillity at first; yet now, even though he had only been up an hour, his euphoria was already eluding him. The harder he tried to catch it the more it wriggled out of his grasp; his pleasure, his sense of power, was so agile that it ran away from him laughing, looking back to see how close he was to catching up; then it vaulted gracefully out of reach and, no matter how carefully he stalked it, drained away through a leak in his mind as expertly as a goldfish slipping through the fingers of a child.

He needed happiness more than ever just now, too, because the immediate past seeping through him was going bad. Like everything that was bad the trouble required contemplation, the balm of re-experienced achievement to soothe it away; for the only way to coat doubt over lay in satisfactory feelings and explanations.

All the same, though, anxiety, barely out of sight, waited to jump him as he searched for his capricious happiness; he felt despair coming for him. He muttered, to ward it off: *Remember the orgasm* – but it was already as flat as a postcard. All that preparation, the deferred, languorous anticipation, and it had still gone wrong somehow. He blamed everything on Flora, but that didn't help. She was beyond his reach now; otherwise he would gently have chided her, scanning her face for any signs that his spell over her was not working.

Yet for the time being at least he managed to go on whispering to himself as if nothing were the matter and he were not out of sorts at all, giving his tie yet another formal twitch, pinching his cheeks to bring colour into them and whistling on at the bedroom mirror. But he was conscious of a void inside him nonetheless, a depression as menacing to his ego as a gash in the side of a boat.

Three weeks previously he had met Ann Meredith in the Anguria, an Italian bar in Soho. It had been love at first sight, and from that moment on his desire for her had driven him as fiercely as the love-pangs of a young man which meant, sadly, that Flora's time was over; she must be displaced even before she was gone. But it was impossible for him to put any of his feverish plans for Ann into action yet, it was too soon; therefore, to distract himself from his fantasies of her, and because the pangs of desire they aroused in him were so sharp that they physically hurt him, he spread his hands in front of the mirror in a wry, self-deprecating gesture of resignation and tried to think about something else. But nothing came to mind except an evening he had spent recently with a book he had found on handwriting, and his surprise at finding that his writing bore the classic signs of a psychopath; Flora and he had laughed out loud over it as he hurled the book jocularly across the room. But inwardly he was worried, for he had to admit that quite often now, especially when he was on the edge of sleep, he was aware of something like a small diseased animal burrowing in his brain, patiently carrying on some obscure kind of work there.

He smiled into the mirror but it didn't succeed. Undeceived, his eyes looked back at him coldly as he told them, winking: *You two haven't seen me out of the wood yet! We still haven't found out how to deal with each other, not even after all these years!*

He was dissatisfied with his face today; it gazed at him, sallow and without expression. He pinched it and narrowed his eyes, but they — even though women insisted that they were 'mysterious, an artist's eyes, Ronnie' — looked back through him flatly, at a flat world; he meant no more to his own eyes than anyone else did. Subaqueous, the eyes of a detached watcher in the depths of a lake, they were not interested in him but in the past; they were still reliving and cautiously catching up with the chaotic situation of a few hours previously.

He tried to correct their lacklustre glaze, but it was a waste of time. Their inky dispassion, his smile, his stereotyped views — mastered and learned by heart in jail — on art, death and relationships, formed part of a fixed set of gestures and passed for wisdom; any attempt to tamper with them contradicted his mask, which immediately loosened, threatening to slip aside like a scrap of plastic dangling from the ear of a drunk. The only reassurance he could extract was the knowledge that the mask had never betrayed him yet; it had deceived all his victims, beckoning them archly into a *trompe-l'oeil* parlour of sanity, when in reality he was staggering to keep his balance in the roaring slipstream of events, clutching the mantle of his self-mastery round him in the frozen delirium of hatred, living to the limit only at the apex of the death he brought the other, and dead to the world thereafter, as well as before.

Without warning, strident music struck up in his brain like the jangling of a banjo in the hands of a disturbed child; voices strode about in his head shouting, roaring out incomprehensible orders. The experience reached a crescendo until a massed, untuned band was sawing, blowing and droning inside his skull; he stood still, shutting his eyes until it stopped. This it did as he remembered how, in a dark West End bar, he had overheard a man he knew was a detective saying: 'What I can never match is the concentration a killer brings to what he does. Whatever I do, his mania leaves me looking ordinary.' Jidney derived permanent satisfaction from that; the opinion of his enemy confirmed his own and he remembered it now with joy.

He turned back to the mirror again: 'Let's go out,' he whispered to it.

He looked anonymous; that pleased him. That was how he wanted to look; you had to take pains to look normal. As he had often said to Flora, and before her to Anna, Mandy Cronin, Judith Parkes and others, one of the greatest attributes of a god is that he condescends to resemble man. Nothing could take this rapture from him – he soared at the topmost flight of existence, he was a super-being. Oblivious that he was a living nightmare he thought only of how important it was for him to relax after the exhausting events of last night, so he sucked air noisily into his lungs, concentrating on the image of his mind as a giant's body – flesh, muscles, sinews, courage and resolve swelled mightily as the precious oxygen of affirmation bubbled through.

He locked up and went downstairs, putting on a sprightly energetic step, forcing his body rather, and aware of a tight sensation in his head. He walked out into the street, still whistling, and turned left up Thoroughgood Road towards the tube station.

And yet his whistling was shrill, because he still felt haunted, pursued even, wondering when he had last had good dreams. 'What?' he thought. 'Still moping over her? Even though she's wept herself dry?' He felt a fleeting regret for Flora, the faint sadness a man might have for some minor loss suffered years ago – a fingertip, or the hearing in one ear.

He sighed, jiggling his testicles in his pocket, on the brink of arousal all over again at the thought of her: *All the same – what memories!*

Memory could be dangerous, though. It was well trained – indeed it was usually as subservient as a footman – but he never really trusted it even so, faced as he was with the daily and virtually insoluble problem of having to forget whole tracts of what he remembered. His memory took him unawares when he least expected it, playing tricks on him, suggesting in the indistinct voices of the dying that he was utterly unlike what he was determined to be in other people's eyes. Where he wanted memory, like a serf, to bring him his version of the past like a brand new coat, it would arrive instead holding something sodden and bloody which bore no relation whatever to the elegant garment he wanted to shrug on. Yet there it was, appearing unbidden with this disintegrating bundle of filth, humid as a shroud, foul-smelling as if someone had left shit in the pockets, offering it to him and insisting deferentially that it was his. Thus memory in its gentle, terrible way translated his own soaring, orchestrated vision of his activities into straight fact, blunt, unsparing and direct, disclosing the infinite to him as a chasm that was terrifying in the extreme; for instead of dutifully confirming the majesty of what he had done it came up with a crazy pile of bones swilling under decaying blood – a version which completely undermined his glittering structure of the past and reduced it to a shambles.

He sang under his breath, in desperation:

> 'Oh just remember this,
> A kiss is still a kiss,
> A sigh is still a sigh . . .'

He pattered on, his lips moving as he walked: 'Oh kissable you . . . How glad I am I spent the whole of our last day with you, Flora. You told me such beautiful and enduring things; not many people can ever have had such wonderful things said to them. And you can be sure that everything I told you as we parted is true; you were wrong to give me such a disappointed look as we separated.' He knew it was all lies. 'I shall do as I told you I would while we discussed *Us* together, cheek to cheek, I shall review our position daily with its sadness and joy – I shall always find time to put myself in your place and say: *Now what, I wonder, would my Flora have done, in this or that situation?*

'Until the very last moment you raised me in my self-esteem; but then you criticised me – so that then, sadly, it became necessary for us to take sudden leave of each other.

'What a strange time that last night of ours was, Flora! The only jarring detail was the sperm; I thought it looked wrong as I left, as if a slug had crawled over a lettuce; it left a sadness in me, and I'm sorry now that the fruit of love's joy went all over the place like that. Well anyway, here I am, back again in our nest, and I felt you last night somewhere nearby to welcome me on my return. As for me, the least I can say is that the "Event" didn't just "go off all right", you know – it was a *triumph*!

'Indeed, my sweetest and loveliest Flora, I never was more pleased with you in my life than I was last night, and I can only hope that the love I have for you shone through my every word and gesture during the foreplay leading to our union – oh, how I *hope* so!' (This was much better.) 'Nothing I did seemed to be pressing you or forcing you, did it? Nothing in my behaviour gave you the impression that anything in our courtship ("Trailing our feathers in front of each other!" Do you still remember how we shared that little private phrase, just the two of us?) was in any way in bad taste, I trust? Something you wrote off as merely some shabby routine on my part?

'And how could either of us ever forget the moment where I said, *Here we are, the two of us sitting up together on our last night?*' (This was quite untrue; things hadn't happened like that at all.) 'And then, when the time came, the way you said: *Now it's all right, Ronald, try to control yourself, please don't be so eager, we agreed I could choose the time – please give me a moment, don't fluster me.* And then, when I had arranged the camera to record us for posterity and you were finally ready, your throat bare, you stretched your arms up like a child bride on the verge of experience, your years dissolving, and said, *Guide me Ronald, help me, be kind.* And somehow I managed to wait, and then you said, your eyes shining up into mine. *Am I the way you want me now? Will you give me a kiss goodbye?* You know, I didn't really want to do that, I was in such a hurry – and I realise now that I kissed you (Did it show? Oh I do hope not!) too quickly and clumsily. But it was the best I could do, and then you said, *Follow me afterwards, immediately, Ronald, the way you promised, I'm very tired now, take me for a long sleep,* so then at last we were united and I found out that I didn't like you at all – I hated being inside you and I remember looking down at you and rushing everything, and it wasn't till afterwards when I took you again – what heaven the second time in spite of the mess! – and held you and said, Oh *my darling, I'm sorry, sorry, sorry* – but of course it was all over by then, too late, and I was so disappointed.'

The great game; how to assemble a million shattered fragments as a presentable front.

He had the film he had made of the scene to look forward to; he had a sudden longing to watch it straight away. Unable to, and ruefully shaking his head in frustration, he left the cramped little stage, brilliant with lights, where Flora was waiting, and instead searched through other parts of his interior theatre, wandering finally into the ground-floor room in North London, bathed in the dark yellow light of its drawn curtains, where twenty yeas ago he had finished Mandy Cronin off. It was just a treasured oldie to set off the fresh magnificence of Flora's act, but yet again, ritually, he turned Mandy's face to the wall because the look in her eyes disturbed him even after he had covered them with her red hair, and stood looking down at her, surprised, while she continued, with the blood-soaked back of her head towards him, to slap her right arm stiffly up and down against her side well after she was dead.

It was a Rembrandt of a scene.

That reminded him of his painting sessions with Flora at Thoroughgood Road; of his sudden great burst of artistic creativity while they had been together. He remembered how he had thought as he stood behind his easel, *I watch your face living, Flora, and paint it dead.* There seemed nothing curious to him in that reflexion, no disparity; he knew simply that he could never let her see the result of his work, no matter how often she pressed him. The point was that fantasies were private; they were destroyed if others saw them.

There were two kinds of time to be. There was safe, and

there was unsafe, or impossible time to be. Present time was always unsafe, future time non-existent. But Mandy and Flora were safe, past time, stimulating time. His self-esteem rocketed upwards.

Free from any unpleasant regurgitations now, he returned to the present and found himself outside Leicester Square station, puzzled and unsure how he had got there. 'Well, why not?' he whispered in the crowd. He smiled at the ground. 'Let's go up to Soho.'

Some Chinese festival was in progress. The Chinese rushed past him, chattering; in the middle of Gerrard Street a diddicoy approached him with a carnation wrapped in foil and offered to tell his fortune. She snatched his hand before he could stop her but only glanced at it before dropping it quickly to say: 'You're not in your right mind.' She made a sign on herself and left, looking back fearfully over her shoulder; her behaviour made him angry, considering he had given her a pound. At first he was outraged that anyone should run away from him like that; then he began fretting that she might somehow have seen through him.

He soon recovered, though, and stared upwards to watch the paper dragons wobbling and curtsying in the wind, their teeth bared as they pivoted gravely to face the fire station. He lingered outside the pub on the corner of Lisle Street; the place was busy. He stood by the door for a while, scanning people's faces, but decided against going in. It was the wrong time of day for him, he liked the dark; besides, he found the atmosphere of that particular pub, with its rock music and smell of cheap cooking, repellent and walked on. Veering towards depression again he crossed Shaftesbury Avenue, still with the memory of Flora as she had looked after he had finished with her – dying, propped against the wall of the vault; pictures of her popped up in front of him one after the other, rich, immediate and stark.

He wondered about the gipsy woman once more, then forgot her completely, because the theatre in his head was brightly lit again and he was back in the vault, sharpening the razor on the heel of his cowboy boot. The razor was not to despatch Flora, only to excite her. He never used the same method twice; like Elgar, he smiled to himself, he liked variations. As for the boots, it was the first time he had ever worn such things. He had bought them to surprise her – they were special boots for a special occasion, a touch of theatre that was also a reminder of their relationship.

For, once he had weaned her from her subscription to the Bible Readers' Fellowship and taught her to worship him, he had sometimes allowed Flora a little theatre; she liked that. After all, she had deserved some effort from him. She had given him her two houses and all her money; in fact she had given him everything she had. She had yielded to him as her new god on the timid condition – as if it were for her to make any! – that theirs was a love to be consummated in the other world where purity had vanquished evil – a secret love, an understood, just-between-the-two-of-us thing like the eye-language between teenage lovers, or anyway the nearest a middle-aged spinster could get to it.

Another case of late passion.

How did he find these women? he didn't know – they just happened. They were childless, well-off and single, submissive and not young, women who couldn't resist looking into the West End bar where he happened to be on a whim, to order a fruit juice and linger over it, perhaps wistfully hoping for a last glimpse of adventure. If they were going to fall for him at all they did so immediately. Women were spellbound by him, positively or negatively; he attracted or repelled them violently and at once, often without even needing to speak.

Perhaps his power came from his eyes. They were deeply sunk, hardly more than sockets in the half-dark of a bar. His lantern face and hair combed back from his forehead gave him an intellectual look which had reminded at least one admirer of Arthur Rubinstein, and it had been almost too easy with Flora really. Her eyes were as straightforward as a proposition of marriage from the first moment, and he remembered yet again how he had hated entering her last night. He belched quietly, re-experiencing his fear and loathing as they joined and she whispered: *We're committed, Ronald.*

This proselytising earnestness of hers had shortened her life still further. It had recurred more and more frequently towards the end of their relationship, so much so that he ended by loathing her as much for her submission as for her strict insistence on controlling her own money almost to the last moment, no matter how much he lectured or wheedled; this was to contradict a god, and in fact she nauseated him so much that, even if it had not been for Ann, he would have got rid of her in short order. In complete contrast to his praise of her a minute before, he had actually got a terrific high as he jostled her without ceremony to her execution, shuffling and hooded from the car to the vault; her intensity, with its jarring vibrations, its troubling undertones of Christianity, inspired a sick disgust in him and released all his power in one ecstatic wave, a fury all the more ungovernable for being long hidden. He had enjoyed her better the second time, when the head was off and that sanctified look of hers gone; he had turned the head to the wall while he detached his relics and quartered the rest, then shovelled it abruptly underground among his other trophies.

And yet, despite his victory, grim shreds of their dialogue still hung from corners of his mind: 'I have a divine capacity to think, Flora; I could have been a painter of genius. I have always known that with my birth a great teacher had come into the world.'

'I want everything from you, Ronald.'

His lips moving quickly, he repeated sections to himself, now, of the usual exordium he intoned concerning the beauty of mutual death; he had perfected the speech, inspired by an Open University philosophy course, in jail. He had delivered it to Flora satisfactorily in the solemn, meaningless spondees of a vicar, but he had gazed at her narrowly all the same as he prepared to straddle her half-clothed body, unsure even at this last moment if he was veering towards bad theatre.

'We are for the splendour of heaven, Flora – we are the fire!'

But even on the night of her death he had not been quite unfettered yet from a sense of his own absurdity and he had gazed at her intently; did she really believe everything he was telling her? With his head on one side he had scrutinised her like a conjuror trying to decide if the member of the audience summoned on stage to help him with a trick knew more about it than he did, though the gazelle had given no sign of resistance. However he was put out and whipped out the Sabatier knife anyway; he could feel his power growing but was terrified that it might ebb, that a chance reaction from her might accidentally lop it.

'Where is death's sting, Flora?'

She screamed when she saw the knife and then, in a fury, after he had failed to penetrate her and botched it, ejaculating between her legs: 'Lie still, fuck you!' he cursed between her wails, swiftly opening her to the heart to observe its last beat, drowning her garbled shrieks and pleas which rose and went on rising until they stopped suddenly, throttled in the tide of her blood, the camera, set up so carefully, turning all the time.

As he was walking up Macclesfield Street his mother suddenly appeared in his head. He snapped her out instantly like a light because what he had been through with her as a child had been too horrible either to remember or forget, but found with growing panic that he couldn't switch her off. She hated all kids and had given him a hard time as far back as he could think, especially when she had a man in the place; usually it was Boy. Now there she was in front of him in a frightful series of snapshots, himself an eight-year-old again dressed in girl's clothes with his skirt up and naked underneath, dancing at the end of the bed while his mother and Boy lay on it roaring with laughter.

He broke out in an icy sweat but the photographs wouldn't stop; he covered his eyes now, in Macclesfield Street, against the sight of his mother's body lying the way Boy had left it after he had beaten her skull in and left. He would tell the police, and later the court, neutrally, as though he were someone else: 'I came back from school that day. I should say it was four o'clock, and I heard them fighting in our ground-floor flat and they were in the middle of the living-room that doubled as a bedroom and I came in to see him holding her by the neck; then he picked up an iron bar, and beat her head in, crushed the top of her skull right in with it, it made a rotten noise, and she shook her head which sent blood flying all over the place and then she went down in a heap, and then he just finished his beer off and walked out into the street.'

But what he hadn't told the police – or anybody else – was that when Boy had gone and he was there with the body by himself before the police came, his first thought had been *I shall never have to dress in girlie clothes again*, and he had edged forward into the room to stare at his mother's blood-soaked body, at her bare belly with the salmon-coloured underclothes spotted with blood and her skirt rucked right up over it. After a time he had approached her; first he had picked up one arm and let it drop, then uncovered her breasts and touched them, then prodded her sex with his forefinger until in the end, growing bold and realising that he wished he had killed her himself, he had forced a piece of kindling into her vagina and twisted it viciously around inside her until his disgust came up and he vomited on the bed. Finally, in a swift movement, he had bent, spat on her and then hit her in the face until her face was gone and there was blood all over him where he had cut his hand open on her teeth.

When the images had at last faded he leaned against a wall in Shaftesbury Avenue. He put his arms round his chest and his hands into his armpits, shivering; by the time he felt better evening had fallen. Clouds stopped over Centre Point, flustered grey hands and driven, elongated faces; they swelled, collected and separated, some with a white plaster gasp in the middle, then raced away on a rising east gale. When he felt able to he turned into the darkness off Dean Street towards a pub behind Diadem Court called The Sicilian Defence – the only kind of defence there was in a pub like that – still physically weak. He had completely forgotten about his mother now because Flora was back again. 'As soon as I've been with a woman,' he thought, 'the moment I've finished with her, it's strange, I see her in a new light – distant, wise in space and time, a true companion.'

Control was everything; it was the long, sure road to affirmation. He pushed the pub door open and walked up to the bar to get a glass of beer.

All at once, feeling uplifted and irresponsible, he decided that 'Biddy' made a fine pally nickname for Flora for old time's sake, for a bit of auld lang syne. He whistled on his way to the bar, changing the words of a rock song:

> Last time I saw yez,
> You shore looked swell to me,
> Opening up your body old body
> To all of my miseree-ee,

> Biddy old Biddy a-ree, a-ree,
> Biddy a-ree a-ree.

'Evening,' he said to the barman, 'pint of Guinness.'

'Stop it, stop it, Ronald,' he said to himself as he watched the glass being drawn, 'you're giving me mind-hop!' He nearly burst out laughing. He shook his head and winked wisely at the ashtrays on the bar; there was just no knowing how a man worked, he told himself.

Feeling in his pocket for a fiver he nodded and said to himself: 'The world is well rid of women like Flora Borthwick.'

2

I was going to see an old mate of mine, ex-Detective-Sergeant Firth, who had rung me to fix a meet; we had said twelve-thirty. I took the tube to Chalk Farm but I was early, so I walked the rest of the way, making for a pub called The Keys of Heaven up Haverstock Hill. Away to the north an IRA bomb exploded and a pillar of smoke rose in the motionless air; presently sirens wailed in the distance and the fire brigade got going. It was December the third and I felt terrible. Good and evil were raging in my stomach, using my liver as a roped-off area, and I was sidling along the edge of a headache; it was also the anniversary of the experience I had got gratefully out of with a DC from another division – I was at the stage where practically every day meant an anniversary of some kind. She had a degree in psychology, and each time we had sex she would say: 'Are you sure you're feeling confident about this?' until by the time it was over I wondered if I felt confident about anything at all.

I didn't mind going to The Keys of Heaven. I don't mind going into any pub when I've some spare time for that matter, just to sit and have a drink and look at people. It hasn't anything to do with being a detective; there's just something agreeable about watching people being themselves, and I never interfere with it.

I don't like anybody else interfering with it either. Indeed I see it as the ultimate point of my job to make sure that no one does, which in our violent and indifferent society isn't easy.

I thought maybe I was going down with a cold. I had woken two hours ago in my flat out at Earlsfield sweating, dreaming I had plunged my hand into a pool of freezing liquid and felt something in there, while behind me a man whispered *I'm just going to climb over into your mind.* It was a grey morning, quiet and bitterly cold with a fog turning to fine drops on my coat; the sun, turning their windows red, weighed over the houses in arms of cloud thin enough to drop it, and I wondered if I had ever really looked at a day at all.

But I would have got up feeling depressed that morning anyhow, because the day before I had been on what Charlie Bowman described as routine business over at Church Road, Leyton. The same evening that he was made redundant the occupant of number forty, a Mr James Boyce, had shot his wife and two daughters dead with a two-two Webley pistol. Hearing the shots, the neighbours had broken the door down, and there was Mrs Boyce with the youngest girl, seven, in the kitchen where the kid had been eating her tea, a boiled egg; all we could really tell from the mother's face was that she had shortly before been crying, though there were no signs of a domestic row. Anyway, having killed them, the widower reloaded (we found the empty shells neatly side by side on the telephone table in the passageway) went into the sitting-room and fired at the elder girl from behind while she was watching the box, the bullet entering the heart; the child looked as if she had fainted with surprise. Then, after writing a few incomprehensible words to say he loved them – the message smeared with their blood and written on the back of his repossession papers which he had used as a flat surface – James Boyce had shot himself. There was a call for his wife from someone called Emma (her girlfriend, as it turned out) on his answering machine and he had left word on it to say they would ring back as they were all just going out. It was a cheerful message, and we worked out that he must have dictated it immediately after the slaughter, as if he hadn't yet quite realised what he had done.

I can't think what they called us in for. There was nothing unexplained about those deaths – unless of course the minister responsible for the economy would have liked to say a word.

That in turn reminded me of a letter I had been shown the other day by the mother of a man I had arrested for murder and armed robbery who was starting a life sentence. He was a postgraduate student in economics, but he also had a thing about stealing antique jewellery to give to his girlfriends. Only this time he had broken into a shop and killed the owner, who had interrupted him, by shooting him in a particularly disgusting way, in the balls, so that the owner, whose heart was weak, had had a seizure and died.

> Dear Mother,
> You used to tell me as a child that the devil makes no image in a mirror; you must have been right because there isn't any mirror in this cell. However, the atmosphere in here encourages me to ask you some questions – I feel sure that, as usual, you have all the answers.
> My questions are probably pointless. Never mind; here goes. Why do I hate women, when I only thieved to please them? Why do I hate being touched? Why do people turn white and seem to die when I go near them? I say *seem* to die because people are hardly more dead to me when I have finished with them than they were before – a lecturer at university once told me it was a

metaphysical point. Why is it that I haven't any sense of humour, as you never tired of pointing out? Why did that lawyer at the trial say that the only feeling I had was in my trigger finger? I only shot the man for a practical reason, because he interrupted me while I was robbing him – and if I shot him badly it was because he called me a dirty word, it was as simple as that.

But some of the others that I'd done before, that I admitted to at the same time to clear the books, some of those struggled, and that meant things got messy and out of hand. Most of them took it easily, but you'd get the odd one that would go on screaming after I'd told him to stop, so I'd no choice but to clobber them more or less any old how. Their screaming got on my nerves because I reckoned it would bring the law down, so I panicked and bashed them around in a way I wouldn't have if they'd co-operated.

I know you always criticised me for treating the truth casually – but there's a reason for that. When other people tell the truth they are admired for it, but when I do it, as I am right now, all I get is the kind of look which I can honestly do without, and I'll let it go at that.

Well, I'm left with the feeling that I've been by myself all my life – in fact I remember as a kid you really did leave me outside the shops all afternoon. What did you do that for? And do you think the results have justified themselves? The psychiatrist here says the images I have of the world lack depth, but I don't agree at all – I assure you that some of the pictures I have of you, for instance, are bloody sharp.

The last time we met, when I was up for sentence, you spoke to me of humanity. Humanity, frankly, is a message that can go out of style. After all, even Christ reckoned there would always be people like me about and he should have known – he was knocked off with a couple of us. The fact that I kill is in fact my whole point

– that there is no point. Everyone says my case is a nasty business, and you spoke up and said I was a total disaster. But I don't believe I am the disaster – I think I'm just a reminder that people are living in one.

Several of the prisoners here have told me they're going to kill me, so they probably will. But since other people's deaths never bothered me I don't suppose mine will either, though I suppose the first night will seem fairly strange.

In any case, even if I do live I shan't see you again for years. We'll both be really old by the time I get out – perhaps you'll be dead even. Never mind. If I write to anyone it might as well be to you, since I both knew you and never knew you – I'm not sure which, because I have never really known anyone anyhow, so it's hard to tell the difference. Do you remember by the way, the time a man came into the house after he had knocked someone over? I've always remembered that – how he trembled while he looked at the body under the car, and his telling you he knew what the void was, and then being sick on the floor.

I've never felt like that. I've looked at the world around me and decided it didn't matter what crime I committed in it – the whole place is the scene of a crime anyway. You always told me to look at the world as it is, and I have.

I shan't do all this porridge. If the others don't top me I'll do it myself. I don't see the end as a threat. I think the real threat is that there threatens to be no end. By the way, a postscript – do look the word 'nihilist' up in the OED before you use it again.

I could see the mother now, as I walked, saying 'I don't know how he came to be in it.'

'In what?'

'In hell.' She meant herself and her son. She looked at

me: 'What would you know about that?'

But what was the point in telling her what I knew?

'To be in hell,' she continued, 'is to be not quite dead. Just not buried.' She stared at a flat spot in her cold, dull sitting-room with the heating off, smoothing her black and white tweed skirt with its dogtooth pattern, plain and infinitely alone, too old to cry, too young not to suffer.

'He's a killer,' she said, 'My Andrew. What would his father say if he knew?'

By chance I had met the father through a case – a man local to me, of definite opinions, who had designed public buildings. As for myself, I felt like Caliban, my love deformed, and no longer young.

'If only it hadn't been for the promises,' she said.

'Promises?'

'If it hadn't been for God. God was a wicked deceit. If it hadn't been for the promises we would have got through hell without even realising we were there.'

'Perhaps the promises are well-founded,' I said.

'Don't be a fool,' she said. She added flatly: 'There's nothing there at all. Andrew's right, hell is resolution in agony, we've all been conned.'

She was middle-class and I was certain that 'conned' was a word she had never used before; yet when she said it then she spoke it as though she had been using it all her life. 'No time,' she whispered, 'no time. Life's like packaged goods, over-wrapped and flimsy – it's hardly believable, by the time you've got understanding it's time to die.' One side of her mouth puckered up the way mouths only do whose owners never knew what it meant to cry.

I walked on up Haverstock Hill with a voice saying: 'My name is Susan Ogdon, I'm forty with no kids; weep for me, I'm a divorced housewife by trade and occupation. Well, one spring morning it was raining, life looked bleak and I couldn't see how things could turn out right, so I took a rope I'd bought and went to a bridge down the road and stood up there with the birds singing and put a bag over my head. I made a double knot in the rope to make sure everything went off right, but I can't have jumped hard enough because I only started to strangle, and that was when I found I wanted to live after all. But I hadn't given myself a chance – I was feet off the ground with no way to free myself, and that was when I understood what the sweetness of breathing meant, when I couldn't. But just then two men from the water came by. They had been sent to cut me off and they cut me down instead – one of them got a knife out of the van and cut the rope while the other lowered me and got the bag off my head – he saw the bag was from the supermarket and said "What an advertisement" as I fell into his arms. I wish he hadn't been married. He smelled wonderful, all oil and metal – first time I'd been in a man's arms for years.'

These memories crowded or sidled into my head together – beautiful, hideous and sad.

Stevenson had a rotten one a few weeks ago, too. He was sent to a house in an alleyway in Kilburn that looked like a side-street to hell because an old man had jumped from the top floor, only he'd had the bad luck to decapitate himself on the fence going down, leaving most of him on the concrete with his bottom stuck up and his bald head a couple of yards away smiling at it. Bowman had sent him there saying it was just a routine matter of making sure he'd gone of his own accord and not been pushed; that way they could close the file.

Later he went upstairs to have a last look round with a local uniformed man; this officer wandered round the deceased's room for a while, looking at the open window the old man had dropped from, just generally looking round. Finally he picked up some of the dead man's underwear, looked into it, sniffed and said: 'Here, look at these, fresh skiddies – fine line in tyre treads, he must have been scared shitless.'

'If you can't master your fear of death,' Stevenson shouted at him, enraged, 'at least don't laugh at it.'

Talking to me and Cruddie later he said: 'There are people who oughtn't to be coppers, or probably any other fucking thing. I don't know. They're just not fit for it.' He added: 'I don't get any younger. I just went away from that place in Kilburn when I was finished. I didn't say anything. I just thought, getting away from that constable who could look into a pair of dead man's pants and laugh, well he's no better than a moron and so much for human progress.' He picked up the file he wanted and turned to us at the door: 'World's gone down the drain, that's all.'

Listening to him I thought, he means people who stop to help someone. As for Stevenson's old man lying cut in two in north-west London, he had jumped in the grim knowledge that for him there was no more hanging on, and he had just helped himself out of the place. The one act of detection now was to realise that London was a war zone. I wanted to tell Stevenson that, but before I got the chance he said: 'See you for a pint later,' and went out. We drank one together later at The Trident. They had 'Just Like A Butterfly Does' on the tape, and the music reminded me of happier times.

Dying. Walking on uphill, I thought dying really was tactless. Death the way A14 saw it didn't just transcend the bounds of taste; it abolished the very nature of taste, striking the definition of nothingness into the hearts of people who spent their lives trying to avoid it. But we didn't see death the way such people did; we didn't see it in a civilised, prepared way. We saw it without the church, without the priest, without the funeral parlour; no hymns, just the dead body, stiffening, sometimes in one, sometimes in more than one piece; we saw death suddenly, when we had a hangover, called out to the raw dank place where death was when we weren't in the mood, like a cabbie picking up a client obliterated by the dark on an empty road. I'm always using memory in my work, as a writer does; I'm after something in the human soul that I can't quite grasp – I read a lot of books in my spare time.

As for Cruddie, he had been transferred to us from Dundee and had to act as a buffer between A14 and Bowman over at Serious Crimes as well as do his other work. Cruddie's last has been the suicide of the wife, just divorced, of the founder of the Gravy Train restaurant group in the West End. Police broke into her flat in Kensington Square because there were complaints about the smell and found her lying on her back with her nether regions dried to the floor by her excreta – she had overdosed on methadone, had a bowel movement while dying and been there five days. Cruddie stopped the car on his way back to Poland Street to buy a glossy magazine for his wife, and there was the dead woman's picture inside with a caption saying how noted she was for her infectious sense of fun and high-spirited talent as a fund-raiser.

And then there was the one Frank Ballard had to clear up once. A man had been queueing in a bank. When his turn came he told the clerk: 'I'd like ten thousand quid.' The clerk answered: 'Wouldn't we all?' The villain shot her dead – she was either too slow in her thinking or a shade too fast with her wit.

The result was the same either way – as Ballard said, never pass an armed robber off as a joke, it doesn't work.

3

I saw the pub a hundred yards away; it was an old building. The upstairs billiard-room had those windows the Victorians thought were the ones people had in the middle ages; the downstairs windows had beer ads set in the panes. The fog was making my right arm ache where I had once been shot, so I put my other shoulder to the door and got into the bar that way.

Firth was a big man, but apart from that he didn't strike you as one of life's success stories; he looked as if he had needed a doctor, never mind a tailor, all his life and had never been near either. He was wearing a grey overcoat with cheroot burns in the target area, and sat with his belly splayed out at an empty corner table with an empty glass on it. The table had beer circles all over it and he was killing a Hamlet in an ashtray; he didn't stir when I came in but gazed at me with eyes like a broken shotgun. He was my age and I had been the best man at his wedding, but now he was that hopeless piece of human waste, a busted copper.

He said carefully: 'I could murder a pint.'

Three years back there had been a night Firth couldn't handle. He had come across a young villain helping himself to a hatchback in Green Lanes and went to nick him, only what he hadn't reckoned on was the bloke coming up to him with a tyre bar and hitting him hard, dislocating his shoulder. Firth ran for it, being on his own, but the wrongo caught up with him just the same and beat the shit out of him, breaking some more bones. After he got out of hospital Firth went back to work convinced he had a yellow streak and from then on, from always having liked a drink, he took to the bottle in such a major way that he had to go.

The last time we met I had told him that although I knew people who drank to hide the fact they were cowards I didn't think he was one. Firth had answered: 'No, of course not. I know. I just drink because I like the taste of the stuff.'

'That's a view no copper can afford,' I said.

'I know,' said Firth, 'that's why I'm not one. However, you've got to have something to take your mind off things, even if they come back worse with the hangover.'

'You ought to think yourself lucky you're out of the Met anyway,' I said. 'No more stabbings, rapes, woundings, affrays, riots, aggravated assaults, first in with the corpse, nothing.'

'You're wrong,' he said, 'I'm sorry I'm out; I've fucked everything up. And then there was Diane – she couldn't take the unsocial hours.'

'That's screwed a lot of coppers' marriages.'

'Diane,' said Firth. He looked into his beer, whistling. 'Remember how you sat up with me the night she left? Me locking myself in the karzy with the bottle of ring-a-ding till you had to come and break the door down? I don't suppose we'll either of us forget that night.'

I certainly wouldn't. I got two pints of beer from a man in a dirty shirt and sat down with him again. 'This your local?'

'A pisspot's local's the pub where he happens to be.'

All right, I thought, so it's self-pity day. Firth had

trouble getting his lips to make words at times, like a man after a stroke. He picked his pint up and drank half of it. He wiped his mouth and said: 'Anything goes, as long as you don't ask me if I've stopped drinking – you look as if you were going to. People do, ever since Diane jacked me in.'

'I've never hated a drink enough to be that critical,' I said.

'I've lost my anger about her now anyway.'

'Good.'

'What's good about it?' he said. 'If you can't get angry about anything any more it means you're over the top and what's more I am – I'm finished, and what the Christ's so fucking wonderful about that?'

I looked at Firth again, thinking of a man I used to see around my flat in Acacia Circus on Saturday mornings who had disappeared a long while back – a fat man in jeans and a double-breasted blue jacket flapping open in the wind who was always shaking with laughter and pointing at people he didn't know. I thought Firth would go that way too if he didn't look out.

Meanwhile the rest of the stuff about Diane was coming out.

'She used to tell me I was great at first,' he said, 'you remember, women's rights, came on strong about how she'd always been a lone fighter etcetera till she met me, and now there I was on the scene at last, a man with an independent mind who washed the car *and* did the dishes but wasn't there when he wasn't wanted either – in fact, a man she reckoned she could settle down with.'

'In fact in the end your own independent mind told you to do as you were told,' I said.

'That's right! I went out of my bleeding way!'

'Never sacrifice yourself for a woman,' I said. 'They don't appreciate it, they explode. I should know.'

'Well, she exploded all right.'

'I can still hear the bang,' I said, 'I was there, remember.'

'That was the night I decided to beat the tom-toms.'

'You poor, half-wide mug, you were way off base,' I said. 'You shouldn't have been beating any tom-toms, you were supposed to be working your cogs off for a bigger car and saving up for net curtains.'

'What about her drinking?'

'You didn't drive her to drink,' I said, 'she flew there solo.' I added: 'You'll replace her one day.'

'Yeah,' said Firth, 'the day Charlie Bowman makes Chief Superintendent.' He peered into the bottom of his glass and hummed a few bars of 'Needles And Pins' into it. 'She's got someone else anyhow, a wanker. Let's have another pint.' When I came back with them he said: 'I ran across them in the street the other day.'

'I hope you were understanding.'

'I was understanding about why people commit murder,' he said, 'if that's what you mean. He's a good deal smaller than me and it was close.' He sighed. 'But then I remembered I'd already got problems, so like a twat I let him go.' He swallowed some more beer. 'Do you remember when she picked up the first dish that night?' he said. 'Started right off with the heavy artillery? Huge great fucking thing – the one we used to serve the roast on when we had folk round.'

'That's right, it had a swan in the middle.'

'That's the one, you remember it pretty well.'

'I should do,' I said, 'it was my wedding present. I found it in Balham market.'

'Yeah, well, where was you then when that one lumbered up the room?'

'Under the table, of course,' I said. 'Where did you think I fucking was? Did you think I wanted to get killed?'

'Well, there was someone else in the bedroom, too, while Di was bowling maiden overs with the soup.'

'That was the man she went off with, the one with the purple Spitfire. Don't look at me.'

'You remember a lot of detail,' he said. 'Too much.'

'Look, it wasn't me in the bedroom,' I said. 'If you recall, I was halfway to the jacks to clean up because I'd caught some spin-off when the spuds came over, and that was when Diane accused me of backing you and that's when I bought the salad bowl as well, beetroot right down my front. I had to throw the shirt away in the death because biological stains are a doddle compared to beetroot, ask any washing powder, and I couldn't have turned up at the Factory wearing that – the villains wouldn't have taken me seriously.'

'Well, I won the chicken and the bread sauce, remember?' said Firth. 'That's when I shouted at her: "Who do you think you are you stupid bitch, War on Want or something?"'

'That's right! And then you drop-kicked the cultural corner – St Francis went for a penalty in the chimney and the third world sculpture finished up in the sprouts tureen. Germaine Greer did the real damage, though,' I added with satisfaction. '*The Female Eunuch* went slap through the hi-fi. You'll never listen to Elton John's greatest hits on that again. Mind, I didn't believe it in the first place when Diane said you'd gone politically correct.'

He said without any warning: 'I'm glad you came as a matter of fact, I want to talk police business.'

'Police business?' I said. 'Christ, I thought it was marriage counsellor's day.'

'Will you just listen?' he said. 'That's all I ask.'

I waited.

'I've got a place near here, pad with a bed, chair, table, cookette, gas fire if you can afford to feed the meter, sixty a week. It's horrible. Still, what did I expect? A castle in Kent?'

'Don't work your self-pity off on me,' I said, 'just ramble on, or else if we're here for a drink let's have a drink.'

A snowflake wandered by outside, kissed the window above Firth's head and melted. He didn't move to go and buy a round so I said, thinking he was flat: 'I can work you a ton.'

'That isn't it,' he said, without thanking me, 'it's nothing to do with that – it's about this man I've got for a neighbour on the top floor. I don't think he's normal.'

'What's not normal about him?'

'He keeps out of sight when no one's watching him.'

'You've got to be extra normal to do that,' I said. 'Maybe he was in the Army. Anyway, if he's that normal, I'm surprised you ever noticed he wasn't.'

'Well you know how it is,' said Firth. 'Once a detective always a detective – you get so used to noticing what's hardly there that in the end you ask yourself if it's there at all.'

'Let's hope that's not the problem this time.'

He let that go. 'He's old, he's about sixty, his name's Henry Cross. He hardly gets any mail and there's no name on the doorbell – I only learned his first name was Henry because one of his girlfriends called out to him on the stairs.' He added: 'And he's got plenty of them. Including the new one, that's number six in the eighteen months I've been there.'

'All right,' I said, 'so he's not a recluse – well, they say the sex drive's the last to give up. What are you suggesting? That these women went to see him and never came out?'

'For Christ's sake,' said Firth, 'do you think I'm saying his place up there's stuffed with bodies? Forget it!' He said with sudden fury: 'Forget the whole thing! I thought I'd got hold of someone with a brain in his head but you're a prick, so why don't you just drink up and fuck off?'

I managed to calm him down. 'Look,' I said. 'Imagine you've got Cruddie or Charlie Bowman sitting opposite you and that you're rambling on like this half-cut to one of them. I'm not taking the piss, I'm putting questions.' I had a hard time keeping my own temper with him and shouted: 'Christ, you know what questions are, don't you? You've asked enough of them. Now get on with it!'

We sat there staring at each other and for a moment I thought he was going to have a go, but in the end he growled something and picked up the story again. 'I noticed these women coming and going on the stairs, idly at first. But then, after the first three, I started noticing them more.'

'Why?'

'I started thinking, we all like to have a go, but it seems a busy sex life for a man of his age.'

'How do you know they met for sex?' I said. 'It didn't have to be for that.'

'Look,' said Firth. 'I've been around, and the way he carried on with them it couldn't have been for anything else. And another thing that struck me as funny: all his women have this in common – they're plain, they're middle-class, and they're none of them young.'

'Could be relatives.'

'Now listen,' said Firth. 'I've got relatives, but I don't go squeezing their knockers and kissing them all over, do I?'

I didn't know what Firth did with his relatives, but I said: 'All right, when he's upstairs with one of these women, do you ever hear anything funny going on up there? Quarrelling, anything like that? No? Well, what's the pattern in these visits, then? Do several of these women arrive together, or one or two at a time, or what?'

'No,' said Firth. 'What happens with each one is that it's always just one at a time for quite a while, and then one day he just doesn't see that particular woman again any more. Not at the house, anyway. He doesn't see her again, I don't, nobody round the place does.'

'Lovers' quarrels.'

'I don't buy it,' said Firth. 'The way Cross does things

is discreet, low-key – every time he brings a woman back with him they go out together twice, three times a week, cooing like turtle-doves, come back to his place over a period of time that'll stretch to two, three months, and then one night, *smack*! He'll go out with her and that'll be it – late the same night or early next morning he'll come back alone, and it'll be the same with woman two, three, four and so on. After one's gone there'll be an interval where he's on his tod and then, bang, along comes another one. I'm not saying there's anything in it – yes I am, I'm saying there's something that smells dead off about it to me. And anyway,' he added, 'I don't like the cunt.'

'Well, if we all started suspecting people on that basis everyone'd be in jail,' I said, 'but never mind, let's have the address of this place of yours – where do you spread the mat?'

'Thoroughgood Road, ten minutes from here. Some of the streets's been tarted up as eighties yuppie, but not twenty-three – that could do with a lick of paint the way I could do with a beer barrel.'

'You live upstairs? Downstairs?'

'I'm ground floor left; ground floor right you've got the Turkish concert pianist (tell me another). First floor left is an old biddy, eighty-odd; then two other old bats opposite. Second floor is two single rooms – bookseller on the left-hand side of the landing, a man in computers on the right. He leaves at eight in the morning if he's been home. Top floor is Cross's place. That must be three rooms knocked into a flat because the centre door's the only one with locks on it; the other two are part of the wall. New lock on the middle door. I know – I went up there one day and had a shufti.'

I thought that if he'd gone to the trouble of doing that then something must really be bothering him.

'How do you pay the rent?'

'Monthly.'

'The landlord come round for it?'

'I never see the landlord.'

'Never? Never even passed the time of day with him, had the odd chat?'

'No, I send the rent in by post – the only time I ever spoke to the landlord was on the phone once about the plumbing.'

'What's his name, anyway?'

'Freddy Darko.'

'That means something to me, that name does,' I said, 'though I can't think just what offhand, which is irritating. Never mind, let's have a description of Cross.'

'He's a cheeky little haemorrhoid,' said Firth, 'he gets right up my nose.'

'So you said. Hold it.' I was thinking about Cross. I went over and said to the barman: 'Have you got a ball-point and a sheet of paper?'

'What for?' sneered the barman. 'Thinking of taking up art?'

'You're spot on,' I said. 'We're up in Hampstead for the day and my friend's got this urge to do some portrait painting. He's convalescing.'

The barman looked at me closely to see if I was taking the piss, but went off in the end and came back with some tired-looking paper. 'I might as well open a bleeding corner shop,' he muttered.

I rejoined Firth, put the paper on the table and handed him the pen. 'I seem to remember you learned to draw,' I said.

'If you call that drawing.'

'Draw me a face for Cross,' I said. 'We can talk while you're doing it.'

'It won't be accurate, just meeting him like that on the stairs.'

'Do your best, it'll give me a face anyway.'

'Mind, there was the night I ran into him in the local

boozer,' said Firth, pulling the paper towards him. 'He gave me a long rabbit about the state the world was in and the soaring crime rate, reckoned all delinquents ought to be sent to penal colonies – he was like a tape-recording of *Mein Kampf*, you couldn't get a word in, and then each time it came to a shout there he was with his glass shoved out, mean as a sparrow's arsehole. And boring?'

'Most criminals are bores,' I said, 'and the moralising ones I've met must run into three figures. They're pretentious too – they think doing disgusting things somehow makes them interesting. So you had to buy all the rounds?'

'Yes, if I wanted him to clack on. Except to my pocket I didn't see the harm in it.'

'Me neither. Did he talk about women at all?'

'I tried to get him to, but he wouldn't.'

'Fancy,' I said. 'You'd think that with all the birds he's got going he'd be keen to show off.'

'I got the feeling he wanted to, but because he didn't really know me he couldn't.'

'That's funny,' I said. 'Not knowing someone doesn't usually stop a bore, on the contrary – and women is the last subject they're careful about. Why shouldn't he have trusted you, I wonder? You never did anything as daft as tell him you'd been a copper, did you?'

'Christ no, I wanted him on full chat.'

'All right,' I said. 'Incidentally, speaking as a copper, does he ring a bell with you?'

'No, but he looks bent enough to have form, and believe me I've thought about it.'

'Think about it some more.'

'I am doing,' Firth said. 'Give me that ball-point of yours, mine's run out of ink. Thanks. No, I can't place him, but you can't memorise every villain in London, your head would go pop. But you could check with Records.'

'Don't worry about horror comics,' I said. 'I'll get on to

them if we need to.' I was still thinking about Darko; the name stuck in my head like a dart in a board. Where had I heard or seen it recently? In a pub? A newspaper?

'Another thing about Cross,' Firth was saying. 'He likes to give the impression he's got no money, but that's just moody – he's not broke.'

'You know if he works?'

'I daresay at sixty he's retired.'

I shut my eyes and smelled banks of faded chrysanthemums: 'Some folks never retire,' I said.

'Are you all right?' said Firth, nudging me. He shouted in my ear: 'Hey!'

'I'm OK,' I said. 'Talking of Cross and money, a flat like that in Chalk Farm, that has to run out at a hundred and thirty a week bottom weight.' I looked over his shoulder: 'How are you drawing his clothes?'

'I'm putting him in his everyday gear,' he said. 'He likes to come on shabby, but I've seen the effort he makes when he goes out with a woman. By the way he's got a car, nothing flash, a Cavalier, G-registered. Christ,' he added, 'I wish we had an identikit, I'm not getting his eyes right, I just can't seem to get them that sunken-looking way. They look as if they were right at the back of the sockets, really weird. Maybe they don't put women off, but they make me feel queasy – I watched him staring at his pint in the pub that night and I was surprised the glass never fucking shattered. Look, I can't rub out, but I'll do another sketch at the side.'

He finished it and said: 'That's a bit better, but they're a real bastard to catch – like water in an indoor well. As for the rest, you can have a look in a minute, I'm finishing off now. Build? He's thin, no all-in wrestler – still, I'd put him at six foot, and a hundred and twenty, hundred and thirty pounds easy.' He pushed the drawing across. 'Here, it's a poxy effort, but it's the best I can do.'

I picked it up. I saw what Firth meant by the eyes straight

away. If he had got the drawing even half right it wasn't a face you would remember unless it really looked at you, in which case you'd never forget it. I put the drawing in my pocket and said: 'I'll most certainly check it out.'

Firth got up and said: 'Good, well that's done. You buying? I'll just go for a leak while you get them – and bring us a chaser with it, a ring-a-ding.'

When he came back he picked up his beer and drank it straight down, then the Bell's, and wiped his mouth on his sleeve. 'Got myself a packet of Glodoms while I was down in the karzy,' he said. 'Just symbolic really, but you never know your luck. They light up in the dark, which is handy,' he added, 'because my dick these days, a woman'd be hard pressed to find it with a searchlight. What a price, though ... Quid a throw, daylight fucking robbery.' He turned his glass round in his hand. 'I was thinking, that's a reasonable likeness of Cross I've done you there after all – it's not art, but it might help you over at horror comics. It's always the same, you notice more about people than you think you do.'

'That's why you used to solve a few cases,' I said. 'Frank Ballard used to say you were neat.'

'A busted detective's free to use his brains,' he said, 'there's no know-it-all snuffling down your neck, it's your one advantage. Another thing, those women, I wrote down the dates I last saw them in case they ever show up on Missing Persons so you can check them – I've got the list at home.' He felt around in his trousers pockets and came up with a dirty fiver. 'Here, it's my shout, but I'd rather you got them in – I had an argument with the governor the other day. I don't know what it is they put in their ale these days, but it makes me aggressive.'

I still had Darko in my head. I said to Firth, 'I've just got a call to make.' There was somebody different behind the bar this time; I reckoned it was the governor.

'Not many folk in here today,' I said.

'It's flat all over. It's the recession, nobody's got the readies.'

'I've seen pubs fuller than this one all the same,' I said.

'Look,' he said, 'I'm Jewish, and if I'm not taking money in this area no fucker is.'

When I asked him where the 'phone was he jerked his thumb at a corner.

'Can I use your directory?'

'Did anybody tell you,' he said, 'this isn't the bleeding post office?'

'I appreciate that,' I said, 'only I can actually see the book sitting there.'

'I'd be more obliging if it wasn't for that pisspot over there you're drinking with.'

'Now don't be judgmental,' I said, taking the directory, 'above all not in a dump like this – when you're running a pub you have to serve all comers if you want to make a profit.'

The governor didn't like that and I wondered if I'd pushed it too far; he had the sort of face that had been in battle often. I was over at the 'phone by the time he got his mouth open, though, so I missed his extremely comprehensive reply.

I looked through the Darkos and found an F. Darko & Associates which looked promising, so I rang it and struck lucky, because I got Mr Darko himself on the line. At that point my luck ran out, though, because the conversation we had was quite strange.

'Mr Darko?' I said. 'Good, I'm trying to get hold of someone called Henry Cross. What's that? You've never heard of him? That's funny. I was told you were the landlord of a property, twenty-three Thoroughgood Road – it's let out as bedsits. Oh, you are the landlord? Well then it's even more peculiar you've never heard of Mr Cross, because he actually lives there on the top floor and has done for several years. What? The name means nothing to you at all? Oh dear oh dear, well, good old number twenty-three – real house of mystery. No, there's no mistake, the name's definitely Cross – unless you know the same man by another name. You don't know him by any name, OK, OK, and what's more you don't give a ... right, and yet you do collect the rent at twenty-three. Oh, I see, you don't collect the rent. Who does, then? A company? What company? Carat Investments. One of your companies? Yes, I'm aware it's none of my business, but there's no need to be abusive – it's just that I need to get hold of Mr Cross urgently. Now hold on, don't hang up on me. Who am I? Well, since you don't know Mr Cross there's not much point my telling you, is there? I just happen to have some information that might interest him a good deal, that's all. Would you be prepared to pass my message on to Mr Cross? You wouldn't. What you mean is that you can't, because you don't know who he is. Yes, I agree, that's reasonable enough, sorry to have troubled you, Mr. Darko, goodbye.'

I needn't have bothered with that, though, because the line had gone dead anyway. I ordered a new round, went back to Firth and repeated the conversation.

'All right,' said Firth, 'well then Cross can't be his real name. Or else it is, only it isn't the name Darko knows him by. Or else Darko's lying.'

'Yes, I like that theory,' I said, 'I think that's far more likely – Darko came on as one of those folk, a ready lie springs to his lips. Still, don't let's get excited. After all, if everyone in this country only used one name it would practically halve the population.' I thought for a while. In the end I said: 'Well, I don't know. As far as I can see, this is what we've got – a man living alone entertains six different women one after the other. They visit him singly over an eighteen-month period; then one evening he goes out with the current runner and comes home alone late that night or early next day, and that's the last anyone –

anyone at Thoroughgood Road, anyway – ever sees of that particular woman. After that he's on his own for a while, then one day he comes home with some other woman, brand new. Aside from that his landlord doesn't know him by the name you know him by, or says he doesn't – and that's it, and there's no crime in any of it.'

Neither of us said anything for a bit.

'Look, I agree it sounds pretty depressing put like that,' said Firth in the end, 'but why don't we just go over to the place? That way you might even get a look at Cross for yourself, or maybe just going there will tell you something.'

'This really has got to you, hasn't it?'

'Yes,' said Firth. 'I know I keep saying it, and I know I can't prove it, but Cross stinks.' He murmured under his breath:

> Where'er you scent a fart, they say,
> A turd's not far behind.

'You ought to give readings from Marlowe like that more often,' I said. 'You do it beautifully.'

4

It was dark when we reached Firth's place. The vanishing year groped its way across North London, smearing the pavements with patches of freezing damp that reminded me of our daily crime scenes, of people who had trailed their broken heads into the corner of a wall and died there.

I got bad feelings about the house the minute we shut the street door behind us. The hall smelled violently of take-away korma and couldn't have looked new even the day it was finished – the staircase neither, with its rotten banister snaking away into the shadows. Firth unlocked his room and left me in the hall while he went to the toilet behind a purple stained-glass door. He pulled the chain and water tumbled wearily after it but he didn't emerge, so I went into his room and got a beer out of the fridge.

It wasn't a room that anyone with positive aims in life would put up with for long. The greasy red carpet was worn through to the threads and I looked down at it thinking that at least the blood wouldn't show when someone cut his throat over it. The wallpaper was the shade of green that only said hello to people looking for a place to kill themselves; in fact it was the ideal surroundings for your end to introduce itself to you in the mirror set into the junk city wardrobe; I expected my *doppelganger* to walk through it any moment with the message that this was it.

Then night closed in with the darkness mankind had coming to it, and Firth made things worse still by coming in and pulling down the bamboo blind.

'Cheerful,' I said.

Firth got himself a lager. After a while we heard steps out in the street and he peered out of the window.

'That's her,' he said, 'the new girlfriend.' He looked a second time. 'Yes, it's her all right.'

'Go out and talk to her.'

He put his beer down carefully and went out.

The front door opened, then shut again and a woman's voice spoke sharply. I moved across the room to listen and heard Firth saying: 'I'm the ground-floor tenant.'

The woman said: 'Really? Let me past, please, I want to go up.'

Firth said: 'If you'd come in here for a minute, I'm with someone who'd like a word with you.'

'No fear,' said the woman, 'I haven't time and I don't know you. Anyway, men don't talk about me.'

I didn't see why. By the crack of light in the doorway I saw she was in her forties, obstinate-looking, and in a business suit, but that didn't make her unattractive. She was slim and her dark hair had some grey in it; one strand had got caught in the icy draught that whistled down the hall and blew across her cheek.

'You're going upstairs to see a man all the same, though, aren't you?' said Firth.

'That's none of your business.' She looked at her watch. 'I'm in a hurry. I've got things to do.'

'Things?' I said, coming out of the door. 'What things? To do with Mr Cross?'

She looked at me in the stupefied way that no liar can ever manage. 'Mr Cross?'

'You know. Mr Cross on the top floor.'

'Who's he?' she said. Firth and I stood there, looking as

silly as she did. 'It's Mr Drury I'm going to see.'

Firth started to speak but it was me she was looking at. 'Who are you, anyway?' she said.

'A police officer.'

She obviously didn't believe me. 'A sleeping policeman?'

'Mind out when I wake up,' I said. 'What's your name?'

'Ann Meredith,' she said reluctantly. 'Miss. Anyway, what's this about? What's it got to do with you who I'm going to see? Are you on duty?'

I was always on duty, but there was no point saying so. She looked from one to other of us, biting her lip; I already found her very irritating. 'Why should I believe you're a police officer? You could be anybody. I don't trust you.'

When she saw my warrant card she looked up sharply. 'Unexplained Deaths?' I was surprised; not every member of the public knows A14 means that. 'Do you know Chief Inspector Bowman?'

'We co-exist.'

She stared at me. 'I know your face,' she said. 'You were on the Mardy case seven years ago; I worked for the defending solicitor. As a matter of fact I was his clerk. I was in court when you gave evidence.' She pointed at Firth. 'And him?'

'Mr Firth's a friend of mine,' I said. 'We want to talk to you, it won't take long.'

'It'll have to be another time. Mr Drury's expecting me upstairs; he'll be here any minute. I just told you.'

'If we could go into Mr Firth's room here.'

'What's the matter with you?' she snapped, 'don't you speak English?'

'I don't want to insist,' I said.

'Then don't,' she said, 'because I know my rights and you haven't any.'

'I know,' I said, 'that's why I'm just asking you.'

'All right,' she said unwillingly, 'five minutes.'

I led her towards Firth's room and she said: 'What are we going in here for? Don't you want to be overheard?'

'You're dead right,' I said, 'I don't.' We got into the room and I shut the door. 'Now then, we'd like you to talk to us about Mr Drury.'

'Why?'

'It's just routine.'

'That doesn't cover it,' she snapped, 'you'll have to be much more explicit than that.'

I counted to ten and said: 'All right, I will be. Mr Firth here used to be with me in the police. He's been living here for eighteen months, and he's been keeping an eye on Mr Drury lately because he's noticed a few things about his behaviour that puzzle him. So much so, in fact, that in the end he contacted me so that we could have a chat about it. And now that we've had the chat I admit I find Mr Drury puzzling too.'

'I can't think why, any more than I understand why you keep calling Mr Drury Mr Cross.'

'Because Cross is a name Mr Drury is apparently using,' I said, 'and that's part of the puzzle. We'll get back to that, but I'd like to know a little more about you first.'

'There's nothing much to tell. I'm forty-one. I live on my own, and I'm with the same firm of solicitors I've always worked for, except that I'm only there part-time now. I don't need to work the way I used to; I came into some money last year when my father died.'

'A lot of money?'

She studied me. 'Two hundred thousand.'

'Have you ever been married?'

'No.'

'Have you any close family left now?'

'Not any more, no.'

'Friends?'

'Besides Mr Drury, a few acquaintances, people I meet at work, that's all.'

I looked away from her because just then I heard a shoe scraping on the path outside the window. Firth must have heard it too, because he looked in the same direction. However the sound wasn't repeated, and she seemed not to have heard it. I said: 'By the way, am I right in thinking that there's no one upstairs in Mr Drury's place at the moment?'

'Not as far as I know, unless he's arrived while I've been in here.'

'Then excuse my asking,' I said, 'but how did you intend to get into his flat?'

She looked at me as if I were a half-wit. 'Well, with a key, of course.'

'So you go in and out as you please?'

'Of course not,' she flared. 'I let myself in by arrangement with Mr Drury.'

'That's unusual,' I said, 'I would have thought Mr Drury would be waiting for you when you arrived.'

'Hen's got his little ways,' she said. 'He likes me to slip in first and tidy up – that's how we always do things.'

'Always?' I said. 'That sounds as if if you've known each other for quite a while. How long?'

She looked put out. 'A month.'

'Long enough to decide you really like him, though.'

'Like him?' she blurted out. 'I love him! He's the most wonderful man I've ever met!'

'Don't his eyes ever put you off at all?' Firth muttered.

'Of course not. I don't know what you're talking about.'

'But have you ever noticed anything unusual about him?' I said.

'I don't know what you mean.'

'His behaviour, say.'

'What an extraordinary question! I just told you. He's the most – well, there are his nightmares.' I could see she regretted that as soon as it was out.

'Nightmares?'

'He has them sometimes. I prefer to forget about them. In fact, I'd rather not discuss it.'

But now she had started it all came out in a burst. Some of them were so bad that they made him jump out of bed. The last time had been three weeks ago when they had been over at her place; he had walked towards the door stiff as a board with his arms out in front of him and she had had difficulty getting him back to bed, calming him down.

'Did he say anything while he was having these nightmares?'

'Nothing I could make sense of.'

'How did he look?'

'You've no right to ask me that.'

'It might be important that you tell me,' I said.

She said in a low voice, as though she were reliving the experience; 'All right, it was just a nightmare, of course, but his lips were drawn back and he was snarling.'

'Were you afraid?'

'I was glad when it was over.' She tried to laugh. 'Poor Hen! Afterwards when I told him about it he made an awful fuss because he didn't remember a thing about it and it worried him.'

I said. 'Have you ever made a will, Miss Meredith?'

She had just started to relax with us, but now her eyes blazed with anger again. 'How dare you ask questions like that! Even from you people that really is the limit!'

'You can't always go by the rule-book when you're trying to help someone.'

'What makes you think I need any help?'

'That's what I'm trying to decide – but I can't help you if you won't answer my questions.' I thought it was so strange, how there are times when two people can't make any sense of each other no matter how hard they try.

She calmed down. 'I had considered making a will, yes.'

'Was that your own idea or were you prompted?'

'Prompted? Why prompted? Hen and I were making plans for the future.'

'All I want to know is if Mr Drury raised the subject.'

'This is intolerable!' she shouted.

'Maybe. But did he or didn't he?'

She flushed. 'Well, we discussed things. I work for a solicitor after all and we drew up –' She looked down at her hands.

'Don't make the will,' I said urgently. 'If it's already drawn up, don't sign it. Or have you signed it?'

'No. It's not ready.'

'Then don't touch it. Anyway not yet.'

'Look, for the last time,' she said, 'will you, in simple language, explain what you're getting at?'

'What he's saying,' said Firth suddenly, 'is that as long as you don't sign any will your health will probably continue middling to good – frankly what he's saying is that once you have signed it on the other hand, the odds in favour of your name appearing on a granite slab look excellent. That's simple language, isn't it?' He added: 'Have you known a lot of men?'

He could have put it more tactfully, but tact wasn't a suit Firth ever led with, and this time she really exploded. 'The answer to your question, Snoopy, is no – not every woman needs to know what you call "a lot of men".'

There again another man might have let it drift, but not Firth.

'Do you go by your instinct when you make up your mind about men?'

'Yes,' she snapped, 'I find it's a very sure guide.'

'That's what my wife thought, too,' said Firth, 'but she thought wrong so she threw the dishes at me and we're divorced now.'

I thought, Christ, he'll be telling her the colour of Diane's hair next. I said: 'How did you first meet Mr Drury, Miss Meredith?'

'By chance. I looked into a bar called the Anguria in Frith Street, and there he was, if you must know.' She glanced at her nails. 'I got on incredibly well with him straight away.'

'Well let me tell you something,' I said, 'you're not the only person to do that. In the course of the last eighteen months five other women have been getting on just as well with your Hen or even better, the last one since he met you. Did you know that?'

It was obvious she didn't, but she rallied. 'Of course I realised he had a past,' she said icily.

'But perhaps not that it was such a recent one,' I said. I turned to Firth. 'When did you last see Miss Meredith's predecessor?'

'Couple of weeks ago,' he said, 'she hasn't been back since.' He added: 'Her name was Flora. I know because I heard him calling her that one night on the stairs.'

That really lowered her in the water; even so, she still didn't sink. 'Hen and I never discuss our past, we accept each other as we are,' she said. 'We love each other. And as for all these questions of yours I know the law, and if you infringe on my privacy any further I shall have them blocked.'

'Don't do that yet,' I said. 'For your own protection I'm going to make inquiries that might need your co-operation, that's all I can say right now. Try to understand, Miss Meredith – police work is as much to do with preventing crime as solving it.'

'You're implying that I might be in danger from Mr Drury, aren't you?'

'I'm not implying anything,' I said. 'I'd rather act on information, only I can't do that if you're not going to give me any.'

'Can I have some idea of what this co-operation might involve?'

'No, because I don't know yet,' I said. 'Maybe there'll be

nothing to proceed on, maybe this whole thing will turn out as flat as a tyre and I hope it does. But for the time being I've got to warn you to be careful.'

'And what if you find you have got something to go on?'

'In that case I'll be in touch with you, which is why I need your home and work address. The phone numbers.'

'This is ridiculous!' she said, but she ended by writing them down for me just the same.

'And another thing,' I said, 'don't tell Mr Drury about this meeting, it's for your own sake.'

Her mouth tightened. 'We aren't used to having secrets from each other.'

'Yes you are,' said Firth. 'He's never told you about his past and you've never asked him, you just said so. So you can keep him in the dark about this.'

'It's completely against our principles,' she said. She looked at her watch again. 'I must go now. I'll think over what you've said.'

'Let me do the thinking,' I said.

'All right,' she said grudgingly. 'As you're a police officer I'll do as you ask for a day or two. But it's absurd, it's like some sort of dream.'

We saw her out and up the stairs. When she had gone Firth said: 'My God, how stupid can people be – two hundred long ones and running about jumping into bed with a total stranger.'

'It's worse even than that,' I said. 'There you've got a woman who's actually trying to die. Deep down she knows she's all wrong about Cross, she knows she's in danger but she just can't help herself, she's too stubborn.'

'It makes you despair,' said Firth.

'Use your time explaining to her about the rabbit and the snake,' I said, 'You've got plenty of it, and keep an eye on her.'

★

We waited for Cross for almost three hours, but nothing happened. 'He saw the three of us talking,' I said, 'he was outside in the street and slunk off, I heard him, didn't you? Pity, I was dying for a chat.'

When it had just gone nine o'clock Meredith came downstairs past our door, alone, and beat on it savagely. She shouted through the panels: 'I don't care what's the matter with him! I don't care! Well, are you satisfied now he's gone? Do either of you men know what it is to be a frustrated middle-aged woman and have a sex life you can finally revel in, no matter how strange it might seem to others? No! No!' she screamed, 'You don't either of you know, you neither of you do, you're cold ruthless blank faceless cruel bastards, and may you both rot in hell, the pair of you!'

It was as though she had been in the room all along and overheard every single thing Firth and I had just whispered.

She went out, banging the street door. It had started to snow. We watched her to the corner; her head was bent under the driving flakes, and she was crying.

5

I sat in the underground going out to my flat at Earlsfield thinking Firth had probably got something. I looked up and down the carriage. People were embarked on the last stage of boredom for the day, the journey home competing with the bad news in the *Standard*.

A Jesus freak got on at Swiss Cottage. He shouted in a high treble voice above the roar of the train: 'Let us all say good evening to Christ!'

No one even said hello. Only the tough little German goddess sitting opposite me took any notice; everybody else immediately got their faces deeper into their reading, so that the speaker was faced with a solid wall of print that ran down the length of the car proclaiming 3 DIE IN BELFAST GUN BATTLE in banner headlines. He got off at Baker Street looking discouraged. I stopped him by the sleeve as he left: 'It took bottle to do that,' I said. I offered him a pound but he refused it, saying: 'Thank you, friend, but Jesus will provide.'

I thought the heavens had worked a flanker on him myself, letting him freeze to death like that – not that I expected a magic overcoat to fall on his shoulders suddenly or anything. When I got off the train I saw two blind men helping each other up the stairs, one of them an old feller who knew the ropes, the other young, uncertain, only just got his L-plates up, probably only just left blind college.

When I got indoors I tried to watch the late film on the box, then gave up, went into the kitchen and got a can of lager out of the fridge. I sat at the table with it under the fluorescent light, but all I could think about was Cross's six women in eighteen months and his nightmares until I couldn't concentrate any more and went to bed.

I dreamed I was driving through a country where I had never been before, slowing up to read a board outside a town too far off to see yet; two roads forked in front of me, one bending off to the left to skirt the town, the other running straight towards it. With some difficulty, because the letters were scaling and faded, I read on the board:

JER. Pop: 1704. Alt: 7 feet.

'Stranger! If you are of no Value to this Town, Drive On. Stay, and you have 1 Week to prove Yourself.

Signed: The Town.'

I got out of the car, slamming the door; the sound was swallowed up in the silent, suffocating heat. I could just guess at the town, a low black smudge on the horizon. I went back to the car and got the map out, something I should have done a hundred and fifty miles back when I must have taken a wrong route off the expressway. I identified a bigger place I had driven through about an hour before as Flensberg, but there was no sign of any town called Jer. There was no left fork on the map either, just the main road that ran emptily on across the plain, parallel with the sea.

The land was nothing but salt flats scattered with a stubble of grass that spread away across grey sand; on my right the leaden water ended where it met the sky. Seaward there wasn't a boat, not even a wave. On the shore there was nothing, either – a lip of shale, bearded with esparto, reached to the ripples at the beach's edge and lapped at it like an animal too sick to drink. Inland it was the same. Not a hill, not a slope even – just bentweed that stretched levelly to the skyline.

I didn't care for what the sign had said, but I had had enough of driving; I had been driving all day, and the car, a clapped-out Ford, looked fed up too. I started walking. I walked past the sign hammered into the ground on its wooden post beside the road and continued on for about two hundred yards; then my attention was caught by a distant movement, and I stopped.

Half a mile off a drab-coloured block, moving in a regular, rippling manner, finally resolved itself, the size of figurines at that distance, as a group of moving men. I went back to the car and found a pair of fieldglasses; I got them into focus, then perched my elbows on the scorching roof of the car to steady myself.

A hundred young men were marching with military precision across country northward towards the town, each with his left hand balancing a boulder on his head. Out at each corner a single man carrying a truncheon loped at an easy double, while a fifth marched out ahead at the front of the group. These were the only unburdened men; the rocks carried by all the others shimmered now and then when the sunlight caught them glittering on veins of quartz. Every man was dressed in overalls the same drab colour as the ground and held his swaying rock on a head shaven bald, the structure of each skull gleaming through its sweat.

As I watched, one man stumbled and let his burden fall; immediately the leader out on the flank nearest to him ran back along the ranks and hit him a smashing blow across the neck. The stricken man collapsed; whereupon, as if nothing had happened, without faltering in their pace to avoid him or even varying their rhythm of march, the others passed over him, the flankmen moving around them in their easy way, until the whole squad, growing smaller and smaller in the distance, disappeared into the haze.

I focused the glasses on the body. It lay motionless on its knees and elbows as it had fallen with its head gleaming in the sun, its forehead pressed into the ground, its rock nearby.

I reckoned the distance between us at three hundred yards, but he looked so close through the glasses that it was as if I were standing beside him. One side of his face was towards me, the part of his mouth that I could see fixed in a grim smile. I swept the area. Now that the squad had vanished there was apparently not a living thing in sight, and I stared at the body while I wondered what to do. The man was dead; it was none of my affair; I had no business with this town.

Only my argument didn't convince me, so I reached into the car for my gun. I thought for a moment, then got a second magazine out and dropped it in my pocket.

I wiped the sweat off my face, crossed the road and started walking towards the body, knowing it was a stupid thing to do. I had no cover, while their people could be dug in anywhere. I didn't know what the citizens meant by values, either, but somehow I didn't think an inquisitive nature was one of them.

When I reached the place I found the flies had got there first. I squatted down beside the body; when I pushed it, it rolled over and sprawled loosely onto its back, face upwards. Its eyes were open and turned up to show the whites, and that was what the flies were interested in. Their scouts were flying lazily round the sockets, also the nose, which had blood in it.

I took the man's head in my hands. The vertebrae in the neck made a grinding noise like a small gearbox not engaging when I moved it, and when I laid the head down it fell onto its left shoulder of its own accord at an angle that made me feel sick. I unbuttoned the top of his denims and placed my hand against the artery in his neck, then on his chest; there was no heartbeat, no pulse.

I was thinking, I can't just stand here with him and accept this situation when I felt the dream ending. I woke realising that the name of the town that the people had intended to write on the board beside the road was Jerusalem, only they had forgotten most of the word.

I got up and made coffee. While I sat in the kitchen with it I watched a beetle crawling along the top edge of the radiator, hesitating on the blank metal face. It lost its footing now and then and paused to recover; I sat watching it for a long while. Finally it slipped again; this time it fell on the tiled floor in a terminal manner, feebly moving its antennae. It waved its many legs continually like blind old women bicycling upside down, its back making a dry tapping sound.

I went over and put my foot on it; then I threw the dregs of my coffee into the sink, locked up the flat and left.

6

I had a problem waiting when I got to the Factory that I had forgotten all about – my name was down with forty others for a lecture by Dr Argyle Jones, the psychiatrist from the Home Office.

The duty sergeant said: 'He wants to see you alone first – you'd better get up there.'

Dr Jones liked these confrontations; he called us in to see him individually from time to time and gave us the results of the checks he ran on us by order from upstairs.

'Sit down,' he said, 'I've had your report.' He smiled past me regretfully, as though he were listening to Mahler's Fifth or seeing a vision. Then he gazed at me and shook his head. 'You're not even trying to deal with your aggression.'

'Right,' I said. 'I need it with villains.'

'Unfortunately it's your colleagues you treat as villains.'

'Some of them are,' I said.

'You've got no sense of teamwork – you've been told that over and over.'

'There's no room for teamwork when you're after a killer,' I said. 'The team arrives afterwards when hell's cooled down.'

He looked at his watch. 'I'm running late. Anyway, your report's gone upstairs; don't be surprised if it backfires.'

'As long as you didn't recommend me for promotion,' I said.

'I'll let you into a secret,' said the lecturer, spinning round in his chair to pick up his papers, 'I didn't.'

So, cutting the blag out, there was my report, and I went off to what was the briefing room before they added a new wing, which we now used as a lecture hall.

I hadn't liked these lectures to date – not because they didn't interest me, but because I didn't think they were what they said they were. They should have been extremely interesting, because they were designed to involve us in an embryonic new programme based on the American FBI procedure at NCAVC, the National Centre for the Analysis of Violent Crime, which had in turn developed VICAP (the Violent Crime Apprehension Programme), a sophisticated computer programme for the profiling and identification of serial killers, the fastest-growing type of killer with us now. I was fascinated with the experiment and watched with close attention the progress of these brand new ideas which were working so well in the States through the archaic structures of the Home Office. That was what the lectures were supposed to be about, but we suspected that, although they were ostensibly an exchange of views between the psychiatrist and ourselves, they were in fact a means of putting us all under the microscope whether we opened our yap or not.

I found a chair somewhere in the middle of the hall, and we waited while the lecturer put his glasses on and arranged his notes. When he was ready he said: 'Well, good morning, gentlemen.' Here he paused, disconcerted, and added: 'But we have a lady present.'

We had indeed – superfit Detective-Sergeant Andrewes ('Where are the other sisters?' Stevenson muttered), the Metropolitan Police champion for the womens' hundred metres. Cruddie reckoned she could beat a squad car on red alert out of Poland Street car park, and shreds of evidence we had put together indicated that Charlie Bowman fancied her rotten.

The lecturer continued: 'Well, apart from the newcomers, the rest of you probably remember me from our last session here together some time ago.'

Some time ago or not, his audience remembered him fine.

'I am going to talk about serial killers today,' the lecturer began, 'I'm going to try to make a very complex and dangerous form of insanity intelligible. You will probably wonder why you find yourselves compelled to waste time listening to me when you've got better things to do, but let me see if I can engage your professional attention all the same in the time we have.'

Somebody coughed and Stevenson lit a Westminster.

The lecturer continued: 'Because of the violence and terror that he has experienced in life, beginning with his childhood, the serial killer cannot conceive of life, whether his own or someone else's, as being anything but violent and terrifying. In his psychic climate, no experience is valid unless it is absolute; secondly, even in his own eyes he is an insoluble algebraic expression, a problem in which there are insufficient knowns for him to evaluate the unknowns. He is deficient in memory, insight, and positive values; and as a result cannot quantify himself, cannot judge either the appropriateness or the scale of his reactions, and is anaesthetised to experiences to which he cannot relate – in other words, he cannot relate to any experience that does not bear a negative value. The experience that this type of sufferer dreads above all is the natural autonomy of the other, because he sees everything except nothing (to put this in the form of a paradox) as being beyond his control. He is unique in his control of *nothing*; therefore his attitude to everything is hostile, threatening, and flat.

'In negative terms, though, the serial killer is remarkably consistent and logical. If the need to destroy is his sole driving force, then he must evidently be devoid of morality;

for although he may be *aware* of morality, his condition dictates that he cannot afford, for reasons of his own precarious self-preservation, ever to acknowledge it. The reason why the courts have difficulty in pronouncing him mad rests, of course, on that crucial word 'afford', because intellectually the killer understands the meaning of the veto on killing perfectly well, even if he is indifferent to it. He is left then with the choice, when directly challenged by positive existence, either to destroy it or himself; for he can neither face a challenge on equal terms nor ignore it. In short, since he cannot ignore himself he is obliged to destroy anybody who might pass judgment on him; there is no middle ground.'

I started to listen; either the speaker had grown up since his last lecture or I had. I noticed Stevenson didn't look as restless as usual either, though he was still murdering the stub of one Westminster filter after another.

The lecturer said: 'I was talking to a killer coming up for sentence on four murder charges and two of rape the other day, and during the course of our evaluation interview he told me: "I dreamed I was hollow and fell. I made a horrible noise falling." I asked him at one point: "Why did you always kill women?" And he answered: "Well, to prove I wasn't one, of course!" "And did you succeed in proving it?" I asked. He said no. He said he had been reading the Bible a lot since he had arrived in prison and realised that he had been born spiritually disfigured. He said he had always been a girl with balls dressed up as a man, so that the manly thing for a girl with a penis to do was to kill women. He said it was that or suicide, and that his method of coping with his unusual sexuality was to dress up and dance in front of a mirror with an officer's cap on his head, spending hours like that before changing and going out to kill. He offered his victim only his "good" profile when he struck; his "bad" profile must never be seen because there was a corner of his smile that had no teeth (in fact he had all his teeth), otherwise he said his personality would collapse.'

'I wish the geezer would get finished,' someone in the audience muttered, 'I've got an embezzlement case on.'

The psychiatrist gazed at him. 'I know you're with the Serious Fraud Office,' he said to the interrupter, 'but I think you ought to realise that the serial killer is the psychic version of a fraud – also that you never know what you're going to get in your work. One minute you're into ledgers; the next whoever you're investigating pulls a gun on you. It's happened. Are there any questions?'

There were not.

Dr Argyle Jones continued: 'In talking about the serial killer we are talking about compulsion. Compulsion has nothing to do with courage. Courage means summoning up the nerve to do something you would rather not do; whereas in a state of compulsion the sufferer (because the serial killer is a sufferer) commits his murders in a dreamlike state, as though he himself were not really committing it at all. Morale in our case means screwing oneself up to do something; morale in the killer's case means living with what he's done, which he does by managing to forget it. Just as the child who wets his bed knows that he is responsible for having done so when he wakes up but wishes to avoid punishment, so the killer is aware of what he has done once he has quitted the sleepwalker's state which engulfs him during the commission of the act – but he avoids the responsibility that he cannot consciously accept by blaming the crime on a mythical *other* which inhabits him.'

He paused to sneeze; he did it stylishly, as if it were a trick he had learned in front of a mirror. Then he pointed at me. 'This sergeant,' he said, 'was confronted with the most bestial case of serial killing in recent British criminal history. I am referring to the Suarez-Carstairs murders, and I have had this officer describe to me how the killer finally revealed himself as archaic, indeed as an archetype of hatred and evil, a face that he had never before shown except to his victims.

Yet Spavento had been running around uncaught for thirty-eight years. I have a comment to add to that.' He coughed, searched in his notes and said: 'An American colleague states, I quote: "It is easy to lose track of a serial killer, because he has developed an uncanny knack of becoming invisible and fading into the background. He has . . . learned how to appear and disappear with as little fanfare as possible."' He looked round the room, took a sip of water and said: 'Archaeology used to be a hobby of mine when I was a post-graduate student; I found that the difference between ancient and modern society was that in the former people looked startlingly different from one another, whereas in the latter they look startlingly alike – which doesn't make your work any easier, does it?'

'We do catch some of them,' somebody said.

'How many times did the police have the Yorkshire Ripper through their hands?' the lecturer asked.

'Nine,' said Stevenson.

'Exactly. The American experience is that the appearance of complete normality in an individual is no reason whatever for eliminating him as a suspect in a serial killing inquiry – apparent normality is the killer's major asset. But once a psychopath always a psychopath – there is no purging his traumas, no cure; he will only add to his record of horror if he can.' He continued: 'Indeed, he must add to it, because the violence he does to the helpless is his admission, repeated over and over, that he himself is helpless.'

I found myself thinking about Ann Meredith. If Cross were indeed what Firth thought he was, then she was certainly helpless.

'Well?' said the lecturer. No one said anything. He looked down the hall and said to a man sitting at the back: 'How long have you been a detective?'

'Twelve years.'

'How many killers have you helped to catch in that length of time?'

'Three.'

'We can't go on like that,' said the lecturer.

Crowdie said: 'If they're so helpless, perhaps you could explain why they try so hard not to be caught?'

'They don't try hard,' said the psychiatrist, 'we only think they do. We think their random choice of victim is a stroke of diabolical cunning, whereas in fact the killer selects that particular victim in response to an uncontrollable impulse. While he is in the process of killing, for instance, he doesn't think about being caught at all – he is in a different world, a state that puts him completely beyond practical considerations like that. He's like ourselves in that respect – I shouldn't think there are many people in this room, for instance, who would wonder if they ought to be putting the kettle on while they were having an orgasm with the girl they were crazily in love with. All the killer can hope is that the planning he did beforehand, during his aura and trolling stages, while he's still able to plan and weigh up chances, will be enough to save him. I repeat – long-running serial killers, the ones with ten, twenty, thirty deaths behind them, are intelligent people. They're often businessmen, musicians, actors, lawyers, skilled artisans, policemen even. But their intelligence is crippled by their compulsion. Are there any questions? Do please ask questions. Do I see any hands going up?'

He did not.

'What you have to try to do,' he continued, 'is to put yourselves in the place of someone to whom fulfilment can only come negatively, through killing – a fulfilment he can never achieve. This failure to achieve is of course precisely what drives him to continue to kill, in the hope that next time will be *the* time. Simultaneously he is also leading the life of a model citizen. But this entire lifestyle is a lie because his destructive actions contradict it – the truth about himself that he has to hide is his profound and total hatred of the human race. He also finds the normal human being incomprehensible; this in turn is a reflection on his intelligence and thus on his self-esteem, which is so fragile that it must be protected at all costs. His answer to this is to convince himself that he is superior to the rest of us – if you like, it is the dunce insisting that he is the brightest boy in the class. Reverting to the question of being caught, such a person is of course terrified of what will happen to him if he is caught, because he will expect to be judged on an eye-for-an-eye basis – as in many countries indeed he would be. But in fact the serial killer is a sad individual, whose every action, killing apart, is a lie.' He began scooping his papers together, adding: 'What protects the killer is his realisation that the bulk of society is humdrum, conformist, and therefore rarely bothered by the police. He has only to hide in that bulk through copying it to avoid detection – remember also that, like a politician or a comedian on television, what the killer is really trying to do is find out how much he can get away with.'

Somebody laughed, and there were some desultory questions. When they had died out the lecturer thanked us and left; the conference broke up and we left too, drifting out into the smell of lunch from the canteen. I remembered suddenly that next week it would be my daughter Dahlia's birthday, and that I must buy flowers to put on her grave. How time passed; she would have been twenty-one. But to me she is always nine, the age she was when my wife Edie threw her under a bus.

As for Edie, I wished she would die; she would be better off than in the place where she's shut up. I never go down to see her any more; they say she's got much worse lately and wouldn't recognise me.

Sometimes I wake in broad daylight and shut my eyes because night seems always to be coming down over the world.

I recalled something my father once told me as a boy: 'Do whatever you like in this world except damage.'

7

I drove down the Baize in the morning to see Darko. The weather had changed. The forecast on the radio was more snow, but right now the sky was cloudless and it was freezing hard. The trees in Hyde Park were rimed with frost, and the whole city gleamed white, gold and silver, as clean as if overnight it had suddenly been purged of crime.
   It hadn't. I managed – for a while anyway – to forget about the crack dealer who had died in the night in cell four. Bowman, with his mates Sergeants Rupt and Drucker, had been getting information out of the man the way Paris detectives call picking the worms out of his nose – in fact his stomach had been mortally jumped on. I thought we had lost Drucker for good when he went to Pretoria on exchange as part of his training for inspector – no such luck, he failed the exam. The positive aspect was that the file had gone right the way up to Jollo, who had turned white because of the current love-your-villain climate and wanted to know if the prisoner had had a solicitor present. Well of course, in the state he was in, dead, the poor bastard hadn't, so that the three of them would be on the fucking mat. The story would stay indoors if Jollo could keep it there; but because Bowman was nobody's favourite and behaved as if PACE was still thirty

years in the future, it could easily leak.

I was going to see Darko because I couldn't see where else to start on Thoroughgood Road. I had read up his past as a petty villain – smuggling immigrants into the country on forged documents and small to medium property fraud. Fred's CV didn't interest me. If he belonged to anyone it was to Alfie Verlander, and I had found Alfie playing snooker in the inspectors' canteen and had a word with him. As it happened, Alfie was investigating Darko right that moment, though he didn't know that yet, and he gave me the story behind the one Tom Cryer on the *Recorder* was running on him, which supplied the detail I had been trying to remember with Firth. Alfie said I was welcome to give Freddy a hard time if it suited me – meanwhile he hadn't known about his connection with Carat Investments, so he thanked me and made a note of that.

Being away from Thoroughgood Road now and also a pessimist, I seriously wondered for a moment if I was wasting my time with it; on a morning like this, driving along Bayswater Road in light traffic with the radio on, it was tempting to write Firth off as a busted copper with a permanent thirst on and Cross as just another old geezer who reckoned he could still get it up. Or it might have had something to do with Christmas approaching – not that that ever changed anything at the Factory except for the worse.

But my euphoria died abruptly with the reception I got when I arrived.

Pyramid Mansions was a block of very expensive flats behind Whiteley's, and I was well started across the wastes of foyer towards the lifts wishing I had a camel and a week's iron rations, when someone with a face like a rifle target and a jacket like a gilt-edged share popped up behind the reception desk. 'Hey, you!' he shouted. 'Yes, it's you I'm talking to! Where do you think you're going?'

His manner pierced the flimsy veil of my well-being like a Serb rocket.

'Hullo,' I said, 'I want to see Freddy Darko, is he in?'

'Mr Darko's not seeing anyone today, and he don't like scruffy people.'

Perhaps this individual had once been a sergeant-major. I walked over to him and said: 'Is that your neighbourly way of telling me he's out, friend?'

He put a finger inside his field-marshal's collar and adjusted his gawky chin over it. 'That's not what I said.'

'So it won't be a wasted visit then, will it?' I said. 'I'm glad of that, John.'

'My name's not John.'

'You look like your name was John.'

'Maybe I do, but it isn't.'

'It is today, John,' I said, 'because I say it is, and I'm on the taxpayer's petrol.' Whereupon I proffered my warrant card, which upset him.

'I think Mr Darko is indisposed today,' he said, 'however I will ring through and see.'

'Miss Otis regrets, does she?' I said. I put my hand over his hand which was on the phone. 'It's all right, John,' I said, 'no need to be too user-friendly, just slow right down and don't be fucking clever. I'm going upstairs now but don't announce me, OK, otherwise you'll be singing Hark The Herald in a treble that'll surprise your whole family.'

I had to work the bell hard when I got up to Darko's flat, but the door finally opened a crack and I stuck my boot in it. 'Any high-fliers at home?' I said.

A face popped round the edge of the door.

'Darko?'

'Fuck off.'

I pushed past him into the sitting-room. 'There you are Freddy,' I said, 'Christ, you're playing hard to find, what are you up to? Rehearsing The Invisible Man?' I shut the door behind me and leaned on it. 'You don't mind, do you?

Anyway I'm in. We haven't had the pleasure yet but you don't give a monkey's because that's all going to change.'

Darko coughed; I soon had him doing plenty of that. His clothes were on the casual side and he probably wasn't in his forties yet, but he hadn't worn well at all. He had an Irish tweed cap on that he didn't even take off indoors; it had a slit cut in the back seam with a pony-tail of flaxen hair poking through it. He must have played rough as a kid, or perhaps it was the booze; anyway he had a nose like a Tuscany mushroom and a mouth like a burst squash-ball.

'Who the fuck are you?' he said. 'More press? I've had enough of you bastards. You'd better use the door fast, mate, otherwise it'll be work for the window.'

'I'm not from the press,' I said, 'though I'm aware you're in schtuck with it – no, I'm from the other, friendly mob but I forgot the flowers, sorry about that.'

'What other mob?' he said. 'How did you get up here, anyway? Through a rat-hole?'

'Nothing to it with one of these,' I said, and showed him my warrant card; I was keeping it busy this morning.

He looked at it, turned pale and said: 'A14? Christ, are you on a death, then?'

'I might be.'

'I don't know about anything like that.'

'You don't know what you don't know till you tell me what you do know,' I said.

'What's that supposed to mean?' He gazed at me in feigned astonishment, like one madman spotting another.

'It means a chat,' I said.

'What, chat to you?' he said. 'What do you think I've got for a head? A popped light-bulb?'

I thought it looked like one. 'It's no good, Freddy,' I said, 'you're going to have to squeeze the brains.' I sat down in a gilt chair covered with Chinese ladies darting in and out of pagodas and looked around. 'Nice place,' I said. 'Pity we can't all afford one – but it seems the only people who can in these hard times are folk who don't pay the rent – eighty-nine thousand quid you're in arrears, aren't you? Oh well, that's democracy.' I sighed. 'Everyone according to his needs, and with a place like this one, Freddy, yours must be pretty special.'

'That's between me and the council,' he shrieked. 'Is that what you've come about?'

'Of course it isn't,' I said, 'don't be so thick. All the same, it's a juicy one, isn't it?' I took out the press clipping Alfie had given me. 'Eighty-nine grand going back to 1990, yet the council's still paying the duke, which it says here is seventeen hundred a week – meantime you're drawing income support on top and you're not even a British subject. I bet they'd like to know how the scam works back in Sydney – my, my, Fred, how do you do it, what's the secret?'

'You do social work in your spare time or something?' he sneered.

'In a way,' I said. 'You know, this is one day where it's fun being the law, Freddy, because I've just had a chat with a mate of mine, Detective-Inspector Verlander over at Serious Fraud, and when I leave here I think I'll go and have another, and then the three of us, you, me and him, can sit down, piece all this hokey together and work out how a few other homeless folk can get in on this fucking thing.'

Darko swallowed.

'But of course you wouldn't want a lot of bother like that,' I said, 'so you might avoid it by giving me a whole load of help on something else.'

'Like what?'

'All right,' I said. 'Now a minute ago I told you we didn't know each other, but that's not strictly true – as a matter of fact we had a lovely rabbit on the phone together only yesterday.'

'I don't think we did. No, I don't remember anything about that.'

'Now don't start losing your memory yet,' I said, 'it's early days and I'm telling you we were, Fred. It was me that rang you yesterday afternoon wanting to know if you were the landlord of twenty-three Thoroughgood Road up in NW1, and you said you were. Which was fine.'

'Yes,' said Darko, 'come to think of it I remember that now. Only of course I didn't know it was you.'

'That's all right,' I said, 'I realise you'd have been more polite if you had. But now we're getting onto things that aren't fine at all and I don't want you playing silly buggers, Fred, so listen carefully and let's get the answers right first time. During that conversation I asked you if you collected the rent from twenty-three Thoroughgood Road and you said you didn't collect it in person.'

'That's correct.'

'The tenants pay the rent to Carat Investments, and that's your company, right?'

'Right.'

'And in particular I asked you then, and I'm asking you again now, if among the tenants at that property you were aware that one of them was a man named Henry Cross. Yesterday you said you'd never heard of him. Now is that what you're still telling me today?'

'I told you yesterday, and I'm telling you again now, I've never heard of anyone called Henry Cross.'

'Now look,' I said, 'I'll try to be reasonable, for a minute anyway, though frankly it's not my style. There's a double order of porkies in all this somewhere, because this man Cross actually exists in flesh and blood – he's existed at twenty-three Thoroughgood Road for years. All right, then, let's put it another way – if he's not called Cross, what's the name of the thin bloke, oldish, about sixty, who lives on the whole top floor at Thoroughgood Road?'

'I tell you, I don't know.'

I exploded. 'Christ! Are you telling me you don't know the names of your own tenants? Do you mean you've got so many tenants scattered around London you can't even remember their names? You will have to do much, much better than that, you little criminal, otherwise I'll have you out in the road with your gear on top of you before you can sneeze backwards in Greek, I'll find a fucking way. Incidentally, how many more properties do you collect rent from besides Thoroughgood Road?'

I saw by what happened in his eyes when I put the question that there was no shortage. 'Bloody mini Robert Maxwell we've got here,' I said. 'Here you are, a hero living on the fat of the land at the taxpayer's expense, and at the same time you're gouging out money all over London – why, it's a scandal!' I said in a threatening manner: 'You do realise, don't you, that just one word from me to Inspector Verlander and you're over the top with this one, Fred. In fact I don't see how we can continue this conversation here, in view of what you've told me. So I think I should like you to come down to Poland Street with me right away so that I can question you further in the presence of your solicitor and other officers.' I reached for the 'phone: 'I shall now call for a squad car.'

'Drop that phone!' he screamed, 'you can't do that to me, what's the fucking charge?'

'No charge – just helping us with inquiries. You'll be out in twenty-four hours if you're clean. But then if you aren't, of course, you won't be, and that wouldn't surprise me at all because nobody, Fred, nobody is ever really squeaky, squeaky clean. Especially not with your record.'

'Now wait,' he said, 'let's keep calm about this and sort it all out, OK?'

'Well,' I said, 'I'm not at all noted for calm but I'll tell you what I will do, I'll give you one more go at this Thoroughgood Road thing. One.'

'Cross,' he said, 'that name rings no bell with me at all, I swear it doesn't.'

I began to believe him. 'How about Drury for a name,

then?' I said, 'does that one work any better?'

'Big fat zero. Nishty.'

'All right,' I said, standing up, 'well as you're all dressed and ready Fred, let's go. You steer, I'll take the pony-tail.'

'No. Wait.'

'Thoroughgood Road, then. Come on.'

'Well, whoever it is,' said Darko, 'if he's paid his rent in through a bank or a post office he'll have a paying-in book and you could have a butchers' at that.'

'You berk,' I said, 'I've got to find him first to look at his paying-in slips, haven't I?'

'I can't see why you want to bother! What do you want to find the geezer for, anyway? What does it matter what his bleeding name is?'

'You're not interested in any of that at all,' I said, 'I'm leaning on you over Henry Cross, so you just concentrate on that. And don't try to be creative, it's not your day.' He didn't say anything, though I could see he was making up his mind to have a try, so I added: 'You've got while I count sixty, starting now.'

'Well,' said Darko after a lot of coughing, 'it's difficult because some of the tenants – all right, then, Carat doesn't always keep records.'

I looked as shocked as I knew how. 'What?' I said. 'Are you telling me you're just taking money from these people and stuffing it in your pocket to go and get pissed on? I don't work for the Fraud Squad, Freddy, but I shouldn't think Inspector Verlander's going to like that when he hears about it, the Inland Revenue neither.'

'Hey, there's a bit more to it than that!'

'Yes, but take the bits away and what's left?' I said. 'As far as I can see, what's left is that cross your palm with silver, Freddy, and good old Gipsy Lavengro here lets rooms and flats on moody agreements to people with any old name.'

He nodded miserably.

'Or even no fucking name.'

He nodded again.

'This is getting better and better, Freddy,' I said. 'So you cop for the lolly, cash, no record, and then just go out and blow it? But didn't you know that's against the law? Know? Do I know what day Christmas is? You are a terrible little deviator, Freddy, and you are in a diabolical lot of bother – it must be your birthday or something.'

'More likely my bleeding funeral,' he muttered.

'Quite possibly,' I said, 'yes, that's highly likely – the way you're going on at the moment you might as well fold up and die. Unless you try a lot harder.'

I sat back and looked at him. Even though he looked like something that had died in a deckchair he was still lying; he wasn't depressed enough yet to be telling the whole truth. Nobody knew better than I did how depressed people looked when the whole lot was finally screwed out of them; it does terrible things to a man.

'Look,' I said, 'what you're saying now is that you don't necessarily know the real names of everyone Carat collects rent from – but although you say you know that whatever the man's name on the top floor of Thoroughgood Road is, it isn't Cross, what I want to know is, how do you know it isn't?'

'I don't know!' he shouted. 'I don't care what anybody's fucking name is as long as they pay up!'

I had an idea. 'All right Freddy,' I said. 'We're going to take a short-cut over this, I'm fed up with it – just dig me up the title to Thoroughgood Road.'

'What?' he said. The sweat started as just a few beads on his forehead; then a big drop of it rolled down his face and spread on his collar. 'I don't keep that stuff here.' He wiped his hand over a face that had been born old.

'Where do you keep it, then?' I said. 'Come on, hurry up. In the bank? In the karzy? Where?'

'What do you want the deeds for?' he said desperately.

'I've just got a sudden passion for them,' I said, 'so I'll tell you what we're going to do – you and I are going round to get them right away, wherever they are. Of course I could go back for the paperwork and make you produce them, but that would be a wearisome waste of time, Fred, and you'd be doing yourself ever so much good if you saved me the trouble. Because otherwise it means a trip to the Factory, only I think a few favours are what you really need just now.'

He groaned; once he did that I knew he was going to spew it all up. He said: 'You're not going to like this, but the title to Thoroughgood Road isn't registered to me.'

I didn't mind it nearly as much as he thought I was going to; the news was like the right click in a combination. I said: 'But you told me just now you owned the place. Are you now telling me all of a sudden that you don't?'

'Yes,' he said. 'That's right.' He looked as if he had fallen out of an old religious painting called 'Resignation'.

'I see,' I said. 'Exit the property wizard, enter the humble agent, is that more like it?'

It wasn't more like it, it was bang on.

'All right,' I said, 'who does own this house, then? How does all this scam work? Now fucking talk. Does Carat own it?'

'Yes.'

'Do you own Carat?'

'No.'

'Are you a director?'

'No.'

'What are you to do with Carat, then?'

'I'm the manager. Look,' he pleaded, 'if you'll just let up for a minute, what I have got here is the accounts.'

'Good,' I said, 'headway at last, let's have a look at those, then.'

He opened a drawer and got out a folder which he pushed across. It was marked 'Carat Investments Ltd.'; inside was a pile of bank statements. I looked through them and found there was a monthly statement for each property. There were four houses, but I was only interested in Thoroughgood Road.

'OK,' I said when I had looked through them, 'only I see the payment's missing for one let on each of these Thoroughgood Road statements – it has to be the top floor. I'm going right back to the beginning of Carat's existence – this one let, no name, no rent received, no records of any kind, no nothing. Why's that, then? Why doesn't whoever lives there on the top floor ever pay any rent? What makes that particular tenant so special?'

'I don't know,' said Darko. 'What happens is I just score one lot of rent from each building a month. I take my commission and wages out of that and then, when I've checked the figures, I pay the balance into Carat Investments, and that's all I know and all I want to fucking know.'

'Well I want to know a lot more than that,' I said. 'Now this phantom tenant at Thoroughgood Road has never paid any rent at any time?'

'Doesn't look like it.'

'No it doesn't, and the question I want answered is why not? Try to look as if you cared, Fred – I'll find out for myself, only the more work you give me the more shit you'll drop into.'

'How should I know? Carat's not worried about it – and if they don't complain why should I bother? Anyway, all I know is what I've told you.'

'It's not nearly enough,' I said, 'it never is with the law when it gets going. So, next – who is Carat Investments? Who owns it?'

He shrugged.

'Don't shrug like that,' I said, 'it really sets me going,

which you don't need. The way you're talking, you'll be telling me next that you've never even met anyone from Carat Investments.'

'You're dead right,' said Darko, 'I haven't.'

Even I was shaken when he said that. 'I just don't believe it!' I shouted.

'Well I'm telling you,' Darko said. 'All I do is check the rent returns, deal with arrears, tenants' complaints, repairs and that's all – what more do you want?'

'A good deal,' I said. 'This, for instance.' I closed the Carat file and picked it up.

'Hey,' he shouted, 'you can't just help yourself like that, where do you think you're going with that?'

'You'll get it back when I've finished with it,' I said, 'that is, if you're not in the slammer – maybe tomorrow, maybe in a year's time, maybe longer than that, never mind. So now tell me how and why you came on as the real owner to start with.'

'That's what I reckoned I'd better say if anybody ever came round asking questions.'

'And has anybody?'

'You're the first.'

'How long have you worked for Carat?'

'Four years – five next June.'

'Think back to there, then,' I said.

'It's a long way back.'

'Long trips are fun,' I said. 'Relaxing. How did you get hired?'

'I advertised I was in property management, someone answered.'

'Who was it?'

'She never told me.'

I was surprised. 'What? A woman?'

'That's right.'

'And you're telling me you don't know her name? Look, your memory is in really horrible shape, Freddy. I don't want to have to play the truth game with you each time I ask you something, it was only fun the first time.'

'I can't tell you what I don't know.'

'Do you mean you never felt uneasy doing business with someone when you didn't even know their name?'

'Oh, come on,' he said. 'You can't be that naïve. If I had to spend my life checking someone's name was Smith every time he told me his name was fucking Smith I'd never get anything done, would I?'

'I'll tell you one thing,' I said, 'you're in a fair way to get some bird done if you don't look out. Anyway, let's talk about money — I might be able to split you off a few bob if you could untangle your brains and remember this woman's name.'

The mention of money immediately made him think; in fact he thought about it so hard I thought he was going to boil over. But in the end he said: 'What's the use? She never figured on any documents, and I only saw her once when the deal was set up, if that's any use.'

It wasn't, but I realised he'd given me all he had. 'All right,' I said, 'but you'd be doing yourself an ace high favour if her name did come back to you.'

But nothing happened, so I stood up. 'All right,' I said, 'don't give yourself a headache, why bother? I'm paid to have them.' I picked up the Carat folder. 'Well, I'll be off, but we'll be in touch.'

'You make it sound like a bleeding seance,' he moaned.

'Don't put your trust in the invisible,' I said, 'you might fall through a cloud, angel.' I paused by the door. 'One more thing — if you've been lying to me, or if you contact Cross on the side you'll be playing with your rubber duck in the showers at Pentonville by Christmas — and that's not a threat, it's a promise.'

He made some sort of noise as I left.

8

My next move was to take the file round to Carat's bank. I introduced myself to the manager and asked if he could spare me a moment. He said he'd be glad to, though I didn't believe him – coppers are like vicars or down-and-outs, they spread a funny sort of aura round them. We sat down together all friendly at his desk, though, and he opened the folder without even asking me how I'd got hold of it. Then he said that naturally he couldn't betray the confidentiality of a client. I said I didn't expect him to, but I don't think he believed that, either, and I didn't blame him.

'How long has the account been open?' I said.

'Four and a half years.'

'Have you or any of your staff ever met any of the people who run Carat?'

'The account was originally opened by a Miss Daphne Hayhoe.'

'Did you personally open the account with her?'

'I did.'

'Did you often have dealings with Miss Hayhoe?'

'There was no need to. It was and is a very stable account.'

'I can see that from the balance,' I said.

That one wobbled into the hedge.

'When did you last see her?'

'Oh, many moons ago,' said the manager. 'Four years ago at least.'

'Can you give me a home address for her?'

'I'm afraid not. She didn't do her personal banking with us.'

'What a pity,' I said, 'I rather wanted to talk to her.'

'I'm afraid I couldn't help you there at all,' he said primly. 'I'm sorry.'

'Don't be too upset,' I said, 'perhaps you can help me with something else. Did a Mr Henry Cross ever fit into Carat Investments anywhere?'

He looked blank. Everyone seemed to look blank when that name was mentioned, except Firth. He shook his head. 'I've never heard of a Mr Cross. You mean Mr Henry Rich, surely?'

That was my cue for a dropped jaw. 'Mr Rich?' I said. 'Who's he?'

The bank manager gave me the smile he reserved for refusing loans. 'You don't seem very well informed, Sergeant.'

'That's right,' I said. 'That's why I'm here.'

'Well, there's isn't much more I can tell you,' he said, 'at least, not unless you show me considerably more authority. I see you're from A14 which is unusual - we don't see many of you. Are you suggesting that this account is linked to a criminal inquiry?'

I told him what I was telling everybody. 'I don't know yet,' I said, 'all I know so far is that a lot of people seem to be living in the same flat at a Carat property and none of them are paying any rent. So let's start again. Is Mr Rich in charge of Carat with Daphne Hayhoe?'

'No. Mr Rich is the sole owner of the company now.'

'Just a minute,' I said, 'there's something here that doesn't quite make sense. Miss Hayhoe, then, where's she?'

'From the bank's point of view she ... well, she just faded out of the picture.'

'Oh I see, and Mr Rich faded in. With Miss Hayhoe's authorisation, of course.'

'Naturally.'

'And then Miss Hayhoe just quit the scene. That's the part I don't exactly understand yet.'

'Why not?' said the bank manager. 'I don't know the details, of course, but as far as I know Mr Rich simply bought her out.'

That was one way of putting it. 'Maybe,' I said. 'Do you have any record of a transaction like that?'

'No,' he said, 'all we've got are the copies of the share transfer certificates which Miss Hayhoe made over to Mr Rich. It was all perfectly straightforward, quite in order.'

'I daresay it was,' I said, 'but I still want to know why it was all in order.'

'Mr Rich was apparently the beneficiary of the whole of Daphne Hayhoe's estate,' said the bank manager. 'The documents came through from her solicitor – it's all ridiculously simple.'

'Of course it is,' I said. 'Put like that, Mr Browninge, it most certainly is simple. I don't know what's the matter with me.'

'You just haven't got your thinking cap on today, perhaps,' he said. 'It happens to us all at times.'

I swallowed that. 'Have you ever met Mr Rich?'

'No.'

'But you've got a specimen of his signature? I might need to look at that later. Anyway, I suppose he withdraws money from the account fairly often?'

'Mr Rich never makes any withdrawals on the Carat account.'

'What?' I said. 'Never?'

'That's right. Mr Darko just charges his fee for managing the properties; the balance goes into a high interest account.'

'Carat pays income tax, of course.'

'Of course. The bank attends to that. We handle all their accountancy problems.'

'Do you have a private address for Mr Rich?'

'Only Carat Investments, I'm afraid.'

I sighed. What the manager was telling me was, you've run into a dead end, mate, have fun. I got up and said: 'Well, thank you very much, Mr Browninge. Have you got any of Miss Hayhoe's solicitor's correspondence on file here, by the way? I don't need to read it – it's just her solicitor's name and address I want.'

'We have it somewhere,' the manager said, 'but I don't quite know if Head Office –'

'I'll wait,' I said.

While I waited, I thought. I thought, here we have three gentlemen with this in common – they can't be found. I had never heard of anyone who went to the lengths to disguise their identity that Messrs Cross/Drury/Rich did. Mr Rich was evidently the undisputed owner of Carat Investments; nobody else seemed to be involved – anyway, not any more. Therefore Mr Rich owned number twenty-three Thoroughgood Road – although Mr Cross, too, enjoyed wide privileges there, such as the luxury of living rent-free on the top floor. 'Hen', Miss Meredith's Mr Drury, also lived there and was going steady with her – just as he had apparently been doing recently with the lady Firth referred to as 'Flora', and very likely, at an earlier time, with Miss Hayhoe too, whose property the house had once been and who had now, having signed every document put in front of her by the inconspicuous Mr Rich, vanished.

I felt that it really was becoming more and more important that I reach any or all of these three individuals and have a word with them as soon as possible – in fact, I was beginning to put a very high priority on it.

9

I had some more waiting to do while I got my Ford unclamped. When the crew finally arrived I said, quite mildly for me: 'You were out of order there, you know, this is an unmarked police vehicle.'

But the senior man on the crew said, as I paid the fine anyway: 'The fact it's unmarked is your tough titty – it was parked on a yellow line and that's enough, there's no use screaming about it, mate.' I'd tumbled on a right comedian here. He laughed his cobblers off as he got down to remove the clamp: 'That's privatisation for you – works, doesn't it?'

'Maybe,' I said, 'but don't stop for a Tango anywhere round here on your night off unless you've made your fucking will.'

Talking of that I drove round to a firm of solicitors called Katz & Katz in Cecil Court, made myself known to the receptionist, and said I wanted to speak to whoever it was who had dealt with the affairs of Daphne Hayhoe.

'That will be Mr Katz,' she said.

Eventually, after a tedious wait of two Westminsters, I found myself in the office of a stout man who was furiously blowing his nose on a piece of yellow toilet paper.

'Mr Katz?'

He gazed at me over the top of his homemade handkerchief, sneezed hard enough to blow a hole in it, and nodded. 'I've got a cold,' he explained unnecessarily. 'What can I do for you?'

'It's about Daphne Hayhoe,' I said.

He beamed and said. 'Oh yes, Miss Hayhoe. Of course! Charming lady, how is she?'

'That's what I was hoping you were going to tell me,' I said. 'This isn't an official inquiry yet and I hope it doesn't turn out to be one, but have you any idea where she is?'

'I'm afraid not. Why? Is anything the matter?'

'I don't know,' I said. 'Your firm does handle her business, doesn't it? Or at least that part of it where she passed her property over to a Mr Henry Rich?'

'Certainly.'

I told him I was taking an interest in Carat Investments and said: 'Could you just explain to me as much as you can of how Carat Investments came about?'

'It was simple enough.'

'A lot of odd things are simple.'

'Why do you say odd?'

'I don't know yet,' I said. 'You know Daphne Hayhoe in person, of course?'

'Indeed I do. Her poor father and mother dealt with us. I handle Miss Hayhoe's affairs myself. I know her well. She's unmarried, an only child.'

'Why poor father and mother?'

'They died together,' said Katz, 'a double suicide, it was very sad.'

'Nothing unusual about that?' I said. 'Nothing that came out at the inquest?'

'No, no. Mr Hayhoe had cancer, and his wife didn't want to go on living without him. The coroner was quite satisfied.'

'Yes. Has Miss Hayhoe any other relatives?'

'None.'

'Does your firm handle much criminal practice, Mr Katz?'

He replied that it did not.

I said: 'It's just a detail – did Miss Hayhoe's parents die before or after the transaction we're talking about?'

'Oh, before. I should say at least two years before.'

'All right,' I said. 'Now tell me about Mr Rich.'

'Miss Hayhoe came to see me one afternoon, and informed me that she wished to pass her very considerable estate over to a Mr Henry Rich, during her lifetime, now, at once.'

'I see. Had you ever met this Mr Rich?'

'No.'

'And did you ever meet him?'

'I did not.'

'You mean, not even at the moment the documents were signed? That seems rather unusual.'

'Not really. His side of the transaction was carried out quite properly, but entirely by mail.'

'There's one thing I want to know badly, Mr Katz. I'm very interested in a certain house. Can you tell me if any property was listed among Miss Hayhoe's assets?'

'I can answer that immediately,' said Katz. 'There was none, apart from the flat she lived in, I think in Chepstow Road. What happened to that subsequently I don't know – but if it was sold the transaction was certainly not carried out through us.'

'Then the street name Thoroughgood Road in connection with Miss Hayhoe means nothing to you?'

'I'm afraid not.'

I somehow expected that, all the same I was disappointed. 'Then what form did Miss Hayhoe's estate actually take?'

'It was virtually all in the form of negotiable bonds, a very large sum.'

'How large?'

'Upwards of four hundred thousand pounds.'

I agreed that that certainly was large and thought there could be the price of two houses in that easily, cash, both of which would doubtless be registered to Carat Investments. 'All right, then,' I said, 'let's get back to Mr Rich again. Do you have, or have you ever had, an address for him?'

'No, just Carat Investments, care of Messrs Darko & Associates.'

'All right. How did Miss Hayhoe seem to you when she first came to see you about this?'

'In her behaviour? Quite normal. I see what you're getting at, though. I tried to advise her – I asked her if she was sure that transferring these very valuable assets to Mr Rich was what she really wanted to do, but all she did was laugh, and point out that at the age of fifty she supposed she knew what she was doing.'

'And you left it at that.'

'Naturally. A solicitor may advise, but of course his duty is to carry out his client's instructions. So I drew up the necessary documents, ensured that they were agreed to, witnessed and signed, and that was the end of it.'

'Thank you, Mr Katz. Do you think you could give me the approximate date?'

He thought for a minute. 'That would have been in June, 1988.'

'Thank you. And was Mr Rich represented by a solicitor?'

'No, I'm positive he wasn't, although I could have the file brought up.'

'That won't be necessary,' I said, 'anyway not yet. But you can see what I'm driving at. I go to the bank that handles the Carat Investments account – no one at the bank has ever met Mr Rich. Next, I get your name from the bank and come round to see you as the solicitor who handled the transaction between Mr Rich and Miss Hayhoe – and it turns out that you've never met him, either. In fact there's a serious shortage of people who ever have met Mr Rich. Tell me something else – once the documents were in order and signed, when did you next see Miss Hayhoe after that?'

The lawyer looked up at me. 'I haven't seen her since.'

'Thank you,' I said. 'You've been very co-operative with me, Mr Katz, so I'm going to tell you something – that's beginning not to surprise me very much.'

After a long silence he said: 'Do you mean you think something's happened to her?' When I didn't answer he added in a low voice: 'You don't mean to say that you think she's dead?'

I stood up and said: 'Why not? Her parents are dead, you tell me she has no other relatives, she isn't married. Carat Investments hasn't seen her, you haven't seen her – who was going to miss her? You didn't.'

10

Barry was sitting with his back to the computer terminal reading his horoscope. 'Mrs Simphonides has got it all wrong again,' he said angrily when he saw me. 'It's not me that ought to be dealing with intractable emotional problems – how could it be when the *Recorder* says I've got Mars in my own sign and that long-cherished dreams are at last becoming a reality? Cruddie says she does a good job on Scorpio, but she can't seem to get Aries right at all.'

'There are millions of Aries,' I said, 'how can she get you all right, and what's the matter with this computer? Broken down?'

'It's me that's broken down,' he said, 'it's the end of my shift.'

'Find me a name before you go, Barry.'

'Look, have a heart, Hendry's playing Jimmy White at Preston in half an hour.'

'Find me the name, Barry – ring Sheila and get her to tape the snooker.'

'Don't you people ever let up?'

'How can we?' I said. 'The villains never do.' I gave him Firth's drawing. 'This is him. His name could be Henry Cross, but it could just as well be Henry Drury or Henry Rich – in fact it could be any bloody thing. See if we've got him, you never know – how long'll it take? I'm just going for a sandwich and I'll be back.'

'It'll take longer than that!' he shouted.

'Oh yes,' I said, 'and while you're at it check if a Daphne Hayhoe has ever been reported missing – age fifty, white, unmarried, probably slipped on the banana skin in 1988. You're a good lad, Barry, thanks again.'

I went over to The Trident, the coppers' pub, and saw Tom Cryer from the *Recorder* crime page at the bar.

'Well, well, fancy,' said Cryer, 'it's been a while, what'll you have?'

'A Kronenbourg, but it'll have to be quick,' I said. 'How's the family?'

'Come and have dinner some time.' He added: 'You've got your working face on, where's the murder? Want to talk about it?'

'No.'

'Anything printed yet?'

'How could there be? There isn't a body.'

'Are you feeling all right?' said Cryer. 'Running after a killer who hasn't topped anyone is sort of new.'

'Don't be too sure,' I said, getting hold of my pint, 'I met one of his future corpses last night.'

'That's better. If there was something in it, would you work it on your own?'

'No,' I said, 'one man couldn't cover it if it took off. I'd have to have someone else in with me, Stevenson if I could get him.'

'Why are you and Stevenson such mates? Because he's another difficult copper?'

'You've got it,' I said. 'That, and I never have to look round when he's there. But lay off it now, it hasn't got going yet. I'll tell you if anything changes. What else is new?'

'We're doing a spread on the soaring crime rate this Saturday.'

'By Saturday it'll have dropped a point, I hope,' I said.
'Going to be your piece?'

'I'm the crime man. The others are all away sunning themselves or getting shot at.'

'I suppose it'll be full of crap,' I said, 'about the public not getting the police it pays for.'

'For Christ's sake don't start,' said Cryer, 'it's lunchtime. Why don't you just wait till it comes out, then you can write to the editor and blast his head off.'

'I just want to know why you write so negatively,' I said. 'Is it just to sell copies?'

'It's the public's right to know.'

'I appreciate that,' I said, 'but do you ever think about the effect that what you write really has on the public?'

'I think about the effect I want it to have. I'm a cynical bastard.'

'You are now,' I said. 'It's a long time since the McGruder case.'

'Why didn't you grow up dirty like the rest of us?' said Cryer.

'Don't think I'm clean,' I said. I emptied my glass and got up. 'I'm off.'

'Regards to the Factory,' said Cryer, ''bye now.'

'Well, Barry?' I said when I got back, 'did you find anything?'

'Nothing on Hayhoe,' he said, 'but your man looks juicy.' He showed me a police photograph. 'This is him all right.'

'Christ, yes,' I said.

'I think so too,' said Barry, 'someone did you a good drawing.' He put a file up on the screen. 'Well, you've got some heavy reading to do. The name's neither Cross, Drury or Rich – say hello to Jidney, Ronald James. Born London 13/4/31 ... children's home 1938 ... apprenticed Wessex Engineering, New Cross, 1945 ... and here we go.

March 1948, Lewisham Magistrates Court, assault on a Jessie Tyler ... bound over ... Jan '49, six months for indecent assault, HMP Gloucester ... national service, August '49, joined under police escort ... January 1950, Barnard Castle, actual bodily harm on Corporal Williams, Military Police, a hundred and twenty-eight days MCE Colchester ... November 1950, Armoured Corps Depot Bovington, arson, damage to War Office property in that he did, to the prejudice of good order and military discipline, destroy 'A' Squadron ablutions block by fire, how the hell did he manage that? ... court martialled ... remanded for psychiatrist's report ... discharged with ignominy ... doing well, isn't he ... April 1956, Bow Street, grievous bodily harm to common-law wife Maybelle Shelley ... four years, they threw the book at him that time ... May 1965, held West End Central for questioning over assault on Gaytime Gondola, I just don't believe that name, prostitute ... November 1966, Knightsbridge Crown Court, indecent assault on Janine Carla Smith, bank clerk, three similar offences considered, eighteen months ... Ealing, July 1967, battery and attempted sexual assault on Judith Anne Parkes, victim refused to press charges ... quiet for a bit ... pops up again, Great Marlborough Street this time, indecent exposure with assault and battery on Sandra Myers, quantity surveyor, 1969, nine months Wormwood Scrubs ... lovely ... then 1970, psychiatrist's report again, draws section six, Broadmoor, two attacks on staff ... released 1975 ... here, listen to this then, 1977, deception and false pretences, also charged with wounding a police officer, Knightsbridge again, five years with full remission for good conduct, that makes a change ... released December 1980 ... served HM Prisons Armley, Canterbury, Gartree, the Scrubs, Gloucester, Lewes, Maidstone, a real tourist ... that's it ... quiet, file ends.'

'Very impressive,' I said. 'I want a copy of that picture

and a print-out of his record, because I want to show all this to the man I'm working with straight away.'

'Who's that?'

'Firth.'

'What?' said Barry incredulously. 'You mean Firth who was busted? You can't be serious. That's not working, it's getting pissed round the clock.'

'I know you used to be married to a clergyman's daughter, Barry,' I said, 'but don't come on moral – I tell you it was Firth who put me onto this, and he was spot on.' I looked at Jidney's face again. 'It's funny. Going by his record you'd think you were just dealing with a crude smash-'em-up villain who's got it in for women, wouldn't you?'

'That's what it looks like.'

'Yes, only the way Firth describes him, Jidney isn't like that at all. You wouldn't think he'd done a day inside; he's harmless-looking, keeps himself to himself except for his girlfriends, he's neat and tidy, no uproar in the house, model citizen. Look at him here at Brixton with his number under his chin. The photo's enough to make God look wicked, but he doesn't look as if he'd topped Grandma even so, does he? Or does he? Anyway, for a man of his age he certainly pulls birds, nice respectable women too, middle-class, well-off, I've met one. So what's his secret? His looks?'

'Christ, no. Look at those eyes.'

'All right then, how does he score?'

'I don't know. Perhaps he plays hard rock through a comb and toilet paper – you can't tell what women will go for.'

'You should know, Barry. And another thing. Normally a criminal's got a pattern – repetitive, stupid. Starts off nicking baked beans in a supermarket – next it's robbery, aggravated bodily harm and on up the ladder till there's a killing. That's the usual dreary pattern, only Jidney's broken it.'

'And he was doing so well,' said Barry, 'graduated through the cement treadmill right up till 1980.'

'Since when he's disappointed us all,' I said, 'nothing since then and here we are in December '92, that's twelve years. So what's he been doing for a living? His wants are modest, OK, but he still needs money for the birds, and he goes for the birds because he has serious sexual problems, look at the file. So what's the answer? Where does the bread come from?'

'He nicks it.'

'Of course he does,' I said, 'but how? Not the hard way any more, no more B and E, none of that, and no more seedy flashing, either – he must be sick of doing porridge, he's got crafty, he's no longer young, he's learned to cool it.'

'So?'

'Well, it's still a theory,' I said, 'but I don't think he ever had just one criminal pattern. I think he's got two, and always has had. He was repeatedly caught on the first pattern, these earlier sexual assaults where he couldn't control himself when he was younger, but they were none of them fatal. But I think on the other, second pattern they were, and are, fatal assaults, and if so he's never been caught for any of them, which makes him a serial killer for gain as well as sexual satisfaction, a killer who's been active for maybe twenty years and a very dangerous man.'

'Why gain?'

'That's to do with a little property company I've been investigating,' I said, 'with the help of a no-hoper called Freddy Darko. Its assets have a mysterious past, and among them happens to be the house where Jidney lives rent-free, would you believe? So if I'm on the right track, Jidney doesn't bother weaving down to Social Security with the old pension book, he harnesses his notion of sexual pleasure to financial need and turns into Messrs Cross, Rich and Drury, three gentlemen with lots of money – in fact so much money that it's not bread we're talking about, it's Mother's fucking Pride. I think he's turned into a sweet little scam called Carat Investments which owns four houses, Barry, houses that were presented to our Ronnie by various female admirers on bended knee.'

'Lucky bastard. No crime in that.'

'Not if the admirers are alive there isn't,' I said, 'no, but if some of these punters turn out to be dead, such as the Miss Hayhoe I was asking you about, then the law is going to want to ask Mr Jidney a lot of very tedious questions which he will have considerable bother answering.'

'It makes a nice story.'

'Yes, doesn't it?' I said. 'The only bit missing is the proof.' I got up. 'And talking of that, I think your Ronald's lovely, I'm a fan – in fact I'm so star-struck that I might go round and see if I can get his autograph.'

'Good idea,' said Barry, 'I should take your cap-pistol just in case.' He shut his terminal off. 'Is it all right if I jack it in and get off home now that I've missed the snooker?'

'You bet,' I said, 'and I'm really grateful, Barry – how about a couple down at The Trident one of these days?'

'I haven't had the five pints you owe me for already yet,' he said gloomily.

'Nor will you,' I said. 'I was reading an article about the effects of too much alcohol on old men like you in the paper the other day, and you want to watch your liver.'

As I was leaving the building to ring Firth a voice yelled out behind me by the passageway that led to the cells. 'Hey, you!' Bowman shouted. 'You've turned up at the right moment, I was looking for someone lying around spare.' He jerked a thumb down the passage towards the cells. 'I've got a teenager in here for throwing acid in an old woman's face and nicking her bag. Come on, he's in cell two, I'm going in to beat the shit out of him.'

'Before you do that,' I said, 'have you ever heard of the custody officer? He's the man who logs everything that happens in a prisoner's day, so why make any more good reading at an internal inquiry?'

He looked astonished. 'The custody officer?' he said. 'What matters round here is that the custody officer's heard of me if he knows what's good for him.'

'There's some legislation been passed called the Police and Criminal Evidence Act,' I said, 'only you've obviously been too busy to read it.'

'That?' he said. 'I've read it, but I couldn't make sense of it somehow, so come on.'

'I'm busy,' I said.

'You've always got an answer for everything, haven't you?' Bowman said, 'that's why I've never liked you, you're a difficult bastard. What do you mean, busy? You're not busy if a superior officer tells you you're not — that's why you're a sergeant. So what are you busy on? A body?'

'That's right,' I said, 'I'm trying to keep one out of the morgue.'

We were walking towards the doors which led to the cells. Bowman looked at the passage wall; there was some writing on it which said: *Lead with your head, man, your arse will follow.*

'It's disgusting,' said Bowman, 'Christ knows how many times I've told them to get this filth scrubbed off.'

'Don't knock it,' I said, 'that's our new democracy.'

'Get stuffed,' said Bowman, 'life's tough at the top.'

'It must be,' I said, 'seeing the way you got there, and talking of bodies, have you, Rupt and Drucker buried that crack dealer yet? Going to the funeral, are you?'

He froze, staring at me. 'Go very easy with that tongue of yours,' he whispered, 'now just be very careful what you say, son.'

I'm silly. Even when I haven't got a reason for doing something, I do it anyway. I could just as well have let

Bowman walk on into the cell where his worried man was waiting but suddenly, I don't know what I thought I was doing, I pinned him against the wall instead so that his headgear fell into a dirty dinner plate lying in the passage.

'What the fuck's the matter with you?' he shouted. 'Have you gone mad?'

I said: 'You know what I'm talking about, I'm talking about last night, cell two.' I kicked his hat off the plate and said: 'Why don't you buy a new one to get fired in?'

He dusted himself off and said in a low voice: 'I'll have you disciplined, I'll talk to you later.'

'There's a lot of paperwork in that,' I said, 'and you mightn't like what crawled out of it, so your best bet is to keep stumm, pretend you're human and think of your blood pressure.'

He turned his back on me and walked off towards cell two. The door of the cell next to it was partly open so that I could hear the prisoner in there saying to the duty copper: 'You wouldn't believe it, but some fucking chaplain's just been round. I said you can stuff that three-letter word of yours, because God's a grass – the only time I ever called the bastard was when I slipped on a roof, and the next thing I knew there was two squad cars down in the street and six wooden-tops.'

What I had wanted to say to Bowman was, before you beat anyone else to death, how do you think thieves, murderers and suicides spend their time? I wanted to remind him that they spend it daydreaming on burst mattresses in a squat littered with old syringes, walkmen burned out on a trip, dust blowing in on the draught under the door, Fuck The Filth! scrawled in the grime on the window, and other men turning over groaning in bursts of bad sleep on sheets stained with their own semen. I wanted to introduce him to the menace of their dreams, of blurred men in watch-caps coming for them, and what it's like feeling for the roach you finished the night before. I wanted to tell him about the sunlight rippling across the walls in the morning as the trucks roll down the motorway outside, and of how their heads crack with the thunder of people with nothing to get up for. Why put your feet into trainers with no soles? Why bother to put your jeans on? The pockets wouldn't hold money even if you had any. That was what I wanted to tell Bowman.

But it's no use telling him anything. He reminds me of a sergeant-major I once busted for an act of gross indecency behind Jack Straw's Castle when I was a young copper on the beat. I didn't bust the man for what he'd done; I busted him because when I tripped over him he informed me he was a warrant officer and tried to grass his partner. There you had another Bowman – the man with the rank who oughtn't to have it. I thought about that sergeant-major when I had the pleasure of arresting him: thank God you wear a crown on your sleeve and not on your head, you bastard.

And that in turn took me back to when I was really small and used to stay with my uncle. I remember one Sunday morning he walked me down in driving rain to The Cricketers pub down Lea Bridge Road and we looked from the thoroughfare across the flats at a place where he said there had been a Nazi 'plane shot down when he was a boy and there was a man who had to run out of the wreck in flames from the petrol. But he had had a few beers by then and went in to see the governor of the place and left me parked by the wooden tables where the trippers sat out in summer with the rain going down my back. I can smell the rain with its promise of spring falling on that big concrete yard still, smell the swollen planks of the tables to this day.

I'm a solitary man. Sometimes, mind, there's happiness in solitude, still, it helps to talk to other people sometimes and dig back together to a time when people felt that the past mattered and something good might happen in the future. But when I open the next door I'm sent to and find the dead inside, overturned bottles and tables, bloody, dishonoured, defamed people lying there, I sometimes accept that dreaming and hoping the way I do is absurd.

Though you never know. A time might come when we all have a direct say in our affairs and until it does, as I tell Frank Ballard and Stevenson the few times we're together, what we have to do is keep going and talk to real people who have some shitty job of their own to do.

I've come to believe that what we need is a republic. People need to be run by people who like them, not boxed into a game they can't win by people who can't lose it. We need a head of state who's been on the run. An interior minister who's had the two o'clock knock and done solitary. A minister of agriculture who's seen a spade fired in anger and done twenty years on the land. A health minister who's had his life saved through swift transportation to a well-staffed, properly equipped hospital. An interior minister dedicated to dismantling the state with its futile bureaucratic waste and saving real money.

And a police force that would put an end to the Bowmans of this world.

11

I said to Ann Meredith over the phone: 'I've got to see you straight away.'

'Today isn't convenient.'

I said, 'It'll have to be convenient.'

I just went on repeating the message until in the end she said: 'Oh God, all right, then. Where?'

'Your place.'

'Is it about Mr Drury?'

'Yes.'

'Is it really that important?'

'It is,' I said. 'Particularly for you. And like all important things it won't wait.'

'You must be able to give some concrete reason.'

I told her part of one or two things that had been coming up; when I had finished she said: 'I don't believe any of it. None of this about Hen. I didn't before and I don't now.'

'Nothing's believable till it happens,' I said. 'See you in half an hour.'

She had to say yes.

She let me into her ground-floor flat in Maida Vale; I followed her into the sitting-room where I saw a perpetual motion clock on the mantelpiece. It had stopped. 'We had one of these,' I said, starting to fiddle with it, 'back in the days when I was married. It was just the same.'

'Well please don't play about with that one. So this is all to do with Hen?'

'That's right,' I said. I forgot about the clock. I found something fat, plastic and brown which growled when I sat on it and passed her the photograph from Records. 'By the way, here's a shot of him I think you probably haven't seen.'

'Well of course it is Hen,' she said finally, putting it down. 'Younger, of course. But he looks awful – what a cheap, nasty camera the photographer had.'

'He doesn't work for *Vogue*,' I said, 'it was taken at Brixton.'

'Brixton?'

'They take one of you at reception. Hen's done a lot of porridge.'

'How much?' she said scornfully. 'Three months? Six?'

'About fourteen years,' I said, 'but I'd need my pocket calculator.'

She swallowed.

'You're sure you've never heard him referred to as Ronald or Ron Jidney?'

'Jidney? What a dreadful name! My Hen? I most certainly haven't.'

'Well as you can see, we have,' I said. 'In fact I've brought you some of our reading-matter on him, too. Take a look.'

She started reading his file, but she hadn't gone far when she turned white. 'I just don't believe this,' she said. 'I quite simply do not believe it.'

'The file goes with the face, there's no mistake,' I said. I would have been sorrier for her if she hadn't been so stubborn; even after what Firth and I had told her she was still like a mouse refusing to see the trap for the cheese.

'If you knew my Hen,' she said, 'you'd see how absurd . . .'

'You'd better get used to calling him Ronald,' I said, 'it's his real name. Has he been in touch with you since the other night?'

'I wouldn't tell you if he had,' she snapped.

'Please don't be difficult, Miss Meredith,' I said, 'it's your safety I'm talking about. I'm going to have to find Hen, and when I do he and I are going to have to have a very long talk.'

'I won't have you harassing him! Leave him alone!'

'That's just what I can't do,' I said. 'If he can explain certain things to me satisfactorily, then that's the end of it – but if not it'll just be the beginning.'

'You'll get no co-operation from me!' she shouted. 'I'm going to get him a good lawyer now.'

'Wait till he's charged first,' I said, 'he may not be – but if he is, it will be with a very serious matter, in which case he's going to need a lawyer badly, and any other help he can get. Meanwhile I want to find him my own way – I don't want a whole load of press and other idiots galloping all over it – that wouldn't help you, either. You don't want to be on page one, do you, that's where they put the bad news.'

'What are you going to charge him with?'

'That'll depend on what this lady called Flora tells me, if I can find her. Or Daphne Hayhoe.'

'And what do you expect them to tell you?'

'To start with, that they're alive.'

She tried to speak, stopped, started again and finally said, spacing out the words: 'I repeat, what are you going to charge Hen with?'

'If and when I've got the proof,' I said, 'it'll be murder.'

'Who are these people, this Flora and Daphne Hayhoe, for God's sake?' she moaned when she had recovered.

'Women who knew Ronald before you did – like the Flora Firth mentioned to you at Thoroughgood Road. I can't tell you any more – all I want to do right now is keep you out of his way because you're in serious danger from him. I wouldn't be here otherwise.'

'You're making far too much of this.'

'For Christ's sake,' I said, 'give me patience, you've read what I've just shown you.'

'I still don't believe it's the same man.'

'I know you don't,' I said, 'even his photograph doesn't convince you, and for a supposedly intelligent woman you seem to have a serious problem with your head.'

'Your problem is you know nothing about love.'

'I have to stick to physical evidence,' I said, 'and I need your co-operation.'

'I don't see why I should help you – anyway, I don't see how I can be any help.'

'It's easy,' I said. 'The first thing you do is a don't. You don't stir from this flat from now on, and you don't let anybody in, either. Not under any pretext until you're properly guarded; I'll try and make sure it'll be a Detective-Sergeant Stevenson. You will do exactly what Sergeant Stevenson says, and you will not answer your phone; Stevenson will do that. You won't go anywhere near Jidney either, no matter what he says or does, because he's going to be very angry. Serial killers don't like being thwarted once they're locked onto a victim, it threatens them in their ego, so he's going to try and get hold of you somehow, and he's a cunning bastard.'

'For the last time,' she said petulantly, 'you're overdoing this whole thing, you've completely misread the situation, this is just melodrama.'

I shouldn't have done it, but I lost my temper. 'Listen, you stupid woman,' I shouted, 'do you want to go shopping for a shroud? This individual has done fourteen years' jail, including spells at places which are just another way of saying hospitals for the criminally insane, and I'm telling you that he's the one most likely to overdo this situation, not me.'

It took me another quarter of an hour before she said in the end: 'I suppose I might stick it out for a day or two.'

'You'll stick it out for as long as necessary.'

'You've no authority whatever to say that.'

'Why don't you ring my Commander, then?' I said. 'I'll give you his extension, then you can have a nice chat with an iceberg.'

'I hate the way you put things.'

'Everybody does,' I said, 'but I don't care as long as I put them clearly.'

'Is your friend Mr Firth going to be helping you too?' I didn't answer because I was using the phone. She added: 'I very much hope not, I get the impression he's an alcoholic.'

The Factory came on just then so I let that slide. I got hold of Stevenson and said: 'Can you drop whatever you're doing and get over here? I've got trouble red-hot here, here's the address, I know because I've started it myself – I'll fill you in with the details when you arrive. It's to do with a maniac the lady at this flat here's got involved with; he'll be after her, so she needs an eye kept on her while I'm running about catching him.'

When he had said he was on his way Meredith said sarcastically: 'Anything else I can help you with now that you've messed my life up, Sergeant?'

'No thanks,' I said. I thought I had never met anyone so obstinately hell-bent on being attacked by a maniac in my life. I held my hand out palm upwards. 'Except give me your keys to Thoroughgood Road.'

'You mean you're just going to walk into his flat?' she shouted. 'You can't do that!'

'I know what I can do,' I said.

That was the end of it. She sat down in a corner of the room sulking till Stevenson arrived; nothing happened in the meantime. The phone was silent. No watch-caps bobbed up in the geraniums; no one in black rubber sped across the garden.

I introduced her to Stevenson. As I left I heard her saying: 'Perhaps that man would be a better detective if people could stand the sight of him.'

12

I got hold of Firth on the phone. 'Listen,' I said, 'I think it would be a shit-hot idea if you and I got together right now, so where's there a pub handy near you? Not the Keys.'

'The Mordred,' he said promptly.

'I know it,' I said. 'I've got a lot to tell you, get over there.'

I arrived first, so I sat in the Mordred having a go at the easy puzzle in the *Standard* until the sun was blotted out by a shadow on the frosted-glass door which reeled inwards, squawking. Firth came in pulling down his sweater over a shirt that was missing a few buttons; he was also wearing a tie in a bright easy-going pattern of squares that made me feel rather like having a game of chess on it. We found a table under the plastic Guinness mirror, I bought two pints and carried them over; then I passed him what I had on Jidney.

'That's him,' he said. 'See the form he's got?' he added when he had read the file. 'I told you he was good news like a flea in your hat.'

'How right you were,' I said. 'We're onto a nice one here, try this for a start. I'll bet you never knew that this Darko you people at Thoroughgood Road pay your rent to isn't your real landlord at all, he's just the agent.'

'Christ,' said Firth, 'do you know who the landlord is, then?'

'Well, yes and no,' I said. 'I don't know Mr Rich of Carat Investments personally, because I've never met Mr Cross, Mr Drury or Mr Jidney – not yet, anyway – but I reckon you must be paying your rent to one of them. In fact you could say you were paying rent to four people, and then again you could say it was only one – it doesn't make much difference really, because here they all are right under your nose.'

'What a bastard,' said Firth, 'paying good money to a man like that. Are you sure?'

'I reckon so,' I said, 'I believe Mr Jidney, Mr Cross, Mr Rich and Mr Drury are all one and the same person. What's more, talking of Carat Investments, I've been doing some research there – Carat doesn't just own Throughgood Road, they've got three other properties, two in Fulham and another in Earls Court. None of them belonged to Daphne Hayhoe – you don't know about her yet – because all her property was liquid, stocks, bonds and cash that she made over to Rich. But your Flora may have been a house-owner, also the other, earlier women he dated. Sooner or later we'll trace everything back through the land registry, but my bet is it'll be a waste of time; the track'll just lead back to Carat and die there.'

'Right now,' said Firth, 'what we need is proof that someone's dead, but listening to you, I don't think any of the original owners are going to need their houses or money back any more.'

'I don't either,' I said, 'so you can see what we're getting into, Ronald's a great one for sleeping partners.'

'I fucking knew it,' said Firth, 'and yet I can hardly believe it. Cross? No one would have thought he had a pot to piss in, but he must be a millionaire.'

'Who keeps the lowest profile I've ever heard of,' I said, 'that's why I want to talk to him so badly. Are you doing what I asked you?'

'I'm sitting at Thoroughgood Road like a spare prick at

a wedding watching what he's doing if that's what you mean. He's out now, or he was when I left. He just goes in and out, nothing extraordinary.'

'That's going to change right away,' I said, 'we're now going to light a fire under him, we're going into the whole of this thing at once. It's risky – still, my career's not brilliant and you haven't got one at all, so we might as well have a go.' I took Ann Meredith's keys to Thoroughgood Road out of my pocket and threw them from hand to hand. 'Are you sober?'

'I wouldn't like to be breathalysed. Why? What the fuck have you got in mind?'

'I hope this doesn't explode – still, don't forget it was you that started it all. I'm going to B and E Jidney's place. I'll have to – I can't go into the Factory with nothing. Why, don't you like it?'

'Me?' said Firth. 'Christ, I think it's a wonderful idea. It looks like the wrong end of shit creek, and you haven't even booked a plot at the cemetery.'

'That's right,' I said.

He shouted, 'Your bloody brain needs rewiring – Jidney could come back any time, while you're in there, and then what?'

'Then the coffin'll have brass handles,' I said. I got up. 'Come on. Let's go straight over to Thoroughgood Road and try it.'

13

'He's still not back,' said Firth, who had been up to see. 'You're all right for now.'

'All right?' I said. We were in Firth's room. 'Of course I'm all right. Even if he finds me in there don't worry – I've got enough questions over Carat to make him seasick.'

'When you're fired remember I never knew you,' said Firth. 'You've got no warrant, you're not ready to take him, you've got no evidence, you don't even know what you're looking for.'

'I'm banking I'll find something that'll connect him to women somehow.'

'I wouldn't give you a hundred to one, and my uncle was a bookie. Get up there if you must, but don't stop and water the flowers.'

'I'll be ten to fifteen minutes,' I said, 'and leave your door open, I might be back in a hurry.'

I reached the top landing and was faced with the three doors Firth had seen. Meredith's key fitted the centre one so I used it and let myself into the sitting-room.

The first thing I noticed was that in spite of the cold both windows were open top and bottom. There was an easel in the far corner opposite, a desk against the wall on my left, a table and chairs in the middle of the room, and a hi-fi, video player and television unit at the back. I was looking at his cassettes on the shelf underneath this when something else caught my eye as abruptly as if it had shouted at me.

An unframed painting stood propped on a table against the wall. It wasn't a good painting. The brushwork was flat, amateurish and crude – in fact it was all the worse for the amount of time and labour that had been spent on it. Yet it was not just a bad picture, an untalented, banal picture, it was an evil picture. Panic, conveyed with a hypnotic power that had nothing to do with art, corroded the subject's face; dread surged out of it with the same archaic power as prayer, forcing me out of the detached role of viewer into that of onlooker. The subject was a naked woman with the thin limbs and flaccid belly of middle age; she stood arrested in a hurried movement against shadows from which the corner of a table protruded out of scale, perhaps the table I was standing by. Enough of the expression in her eyes, which were dark with terror, had been captured to make even me shiver. She was gazing, not at the viewer but behind him, and her mouth was the more alarming because it had not been painted at all – an absence which suggested that if it had been there it would have been wide open, convulsed with a fear that the painter had seen no need to render, and screaming.

Other parts of her besides the mouth, her genitalia, her nipples, were also missing. Her right arm, sharp against the blackness behind her, was horizontally extended; there was no blood anywhere, but in her right hand she held her disembodied left hand which dangled emptily, like a rubber glove. The whole concentration of the painting was in the intensity of her eyes; the rest of her crouched misshapenly off balance, as though to ward off an attack.

At the foot of the painting was the word *Purified*, followed by a mocking face.

I knew I was looking at a murder badly painted by the man who had committed it; I looked at it until I could bear it no longer, turning it face to the wall, and went back to searching the flat. The books yielded nothing; the furniture was the kind you would pick up at a car-boot sale. I looked into the bathroom – nothing. In the kitchen, just one item that interested me – Jidney had left a shopping-list on the table. Graphology interests me; criminal handwriting teems with evidence of caution, unbalanced thinking and deceit.

This certainly fitted Jidney's script, which I found remarkable as an example of both superficiality and aggression. The huge, embellished capitals were grossly out of proportion to the thready, manipulative middle zone which was decorated and enrolled, announcing an inflated but fragile ego supported by manipulative cruelty and coupled with a shallow desire to please. The 'm's and 'n's were arcaded in the classic formation of the fraud, and the upper zone was equally fascinating; the high loops of the 'h's and 'l's were abnormally tall and those of the 'g's and 'y's correspondingly long, entangling themselves in the strokes of the lines above and below, indications of mythomania and a vacillating hold on reality. The letter 'i' was capped not with a dot but with a long dash, a mark of violence, and the general tendency of the lines was an urgency towards the right-hand side of the page where, abruptly and on its own, stood the word 'butter' – here the last three letters reversed sharply into the rest, the bar across the double 't' running backwards towards the 'b' in a single stroke, cancelling the first part of the word, a trait common in the script of assassins and suicides. Between the words 'tea-bags' and 'eggs' I found the drawing of another little face similar to the one at the foot of the painting and present for no reason – a symptom of associative dysfunctions and aural or visual hallucinations leading to sensations of depersonalisation and delusions such as divine commands, orders, and revelations.

I went next door; the single bed in there was narrow and made up; the chest of drawers revealed nothing but clean shirts and socks. It was the same with the wardrobe, which contained two suits, a selection of ties and two pairs of black shoes. However much Jidney was worth, nothing in the place had cost much. I turned back into the living-room and went over to a table in one corner with a telephone on it. I took the number and went through the pad beside it; there was nothing on it but the word Ann traced through from the preceding page. In fact so far, apart from the painting, the flat was remarkable only for being exactly what it was – a place inhabited by a single man of few means. I stripped the armchairs and felt around in the lining. I might as well not have bothered; there was nothing there.

That left the desk. It was a cheap roll-top, and the locks didn't delay me long. There were five drawers, a long shallow one under the writing surface and two each side. There was a leather-bound photograph album in a black binding inside the long drawer full of photographs of women; some posed, taken in a studio, others just casual. The first was a dog-eared snapshot that showed a woman reclining uncomfortably on a grass bank and squinting into the sunlight. There was no date on it, but judging by her clothes and the way the snap had faded, it was at least twenty years old and signed Gerda on the back. All the photographs had names on them somewhere, several of them in Jidney's handwriting.

None of the sixteen women in the album were young. Besides Gerda I met Mandy, Daphne, Janice, Jenny, Judith, Frances, Mary, Christine, Sue, Pat. Flora was there too, of course, and I took the album across to compare it with the face in the painting; the latter was so distorted, though, that it was hard to be sure. I got the names down, memorised the faces and put the album back in the drawer – what else could I do? On its own the album was worthless, a circumstantial link at best; confronted with it, confronted with the fact, even if I could establish it, that these women had been dead for years, all Jidney had to say was 'So what? Are you trying to say I killed them? Prove it.' I looked at the time; I had been in there nine minutes already.

I opened the top left-hand drawer. Folded, and lying under a packet of envelopes, paper-clips and paid gas bills, I found an old letter on HMP Gartree stationery dated 1972 that started: 'Christine, After what I have done to you I don't know how to begin this...' followed by a declaration of love. Here the writing, though it was Jidney's all right, was barely legible compared to the sample in the kitchen; it was so pasty that the spaces inside many of the letters were filled in, written under extreme downward pressure, the words formed so quickly that some of them had run into each other; also, in contrast to whatever sentimental message the writer was conveying, the upstrokes were pointed and vicious. But the decorated capital letters with their ornate scrolling were the same, reminding me of a bad actor trying to dominate a stage, and many of the words ended in sharp downward strokes like the plunge of a dagger. But the letter was no use to me either, so I left it and tried the drawer underneath.

At first I thought that was empty too, then right at the back I saw a rectangular shape under the lining-paper; removing this I found a notebook two inches square. There was a six-digit figure, 713206, on the first page and nothing else – most of the other pages had been torn out. I copied it down in my notebook on the chance that, if I could only decipher it, the numeral and the photographs might somehow be linked, put the book back as I had found it and closed the drawer.

I opened the last drawer and found just one video cassette inside. The box had a high street brand name on it. There was no camera in the flat but that could be anywhere – in a shed, a basement, in the boot of a car. I was just dropping the cassette into my pocket when I heard the street door opening and shutting again downstairs, so I locked the desk and left the flat the fast way, sliding down the banister to the second floor landing.

I passed Jidney coming up from the first floor carrying a plastic bag. We didn't even glance at each other, but I heard him stop on the stairs further up and knew he was looking back.

When I got back to Firth's room he said: 'I saw him go in, you must have passed him.'

'Yes,' I said, 'on the stairs between the first and second floors.'

'Did you find anything?'

'Enough to know we can't go on like this on our own any more – I'll have to straighten it out at the Factory.'

'Are you any further on?'

I told him about the painting, the photographs.

'Photographs?'

'Sixteen women.'

'Check them with Missing Persons.'

'Yes,' I said, 'but it'll take too long, there's the Meredith woman to worry about.'

I showed him the video.

'That's theft,' said Firth. 'If Jidney finds this gone or there's nothing on it but Mickey Mouse you'll have no knackers in your knickers.'

'I'll likely end up with neither anyway,' I said. As I was leaving I showed him the number I had copied down from the notebook. 'What do you think this means?'

He looked at it. 'Nothing to me.'

'Don't worry about it,' I said, 'it doesn't to me either.'

14

It seems a long time ago now since I first met Cruddie. He had been transferred to us from Dundee, and the first morning we ever met was the wrong one because it was my first morning back at work after a week's leave.

'I've got a lovely treat waiting for you,' said Stevenson when I got in, 'he's called – it sounds like – Cruddie, he's thirty-four, single, and keen as shit.'

'You make him sound like Charlie Bowman at the chrysalis stage,' I said. 'What did they have to send him to A14 for when they've got Norway up there dead opposite?'

'He's no Charlie Bowman,' said Stevenson. 'He's no pen-pusher, either.'

'Can't wait to get at a few of our idle southern villains, is that it?'

He threw his empty Westminster packet into the out-tray. 'I'm not sure I'd like to be the villain he did get at,' he said, and added: 'or one of us coppers that got out of line, either.'

'All right,' I said, 'well, what other problems have we got?'

'I don't know about us,' said Stevenson, 'but you've got two. Cruddie wants to see you, that's one, to introduce himself I think is the idea. And so does Charlie – who's bought another new hat to go up to a case in Millionaires'

Row by the way, so try not to piss in it, I can see you're just in the mood.'

Before I could say anything, steps clattered up our cement staircase to the second floor, pounding towards room 202. Stevenson slammed a pound coin on the table. 'Talk of the devil, Charlie.'

'It isn't,' I said, 'you've lost that, that's Eight O'Clock Andrewes on the dot with the bad news.'

Sure enough, Sergeant Andrewes burst in. I collared the pound and Stevenson looked her over wearily. 'You'll never get married wearing boots like that, Deirdre,' he said, 'we couldn't give you away in the prison chapel.'

'You're a dirty lot in here,' said Andrewes, 'and your pitiful minds are in the same state as your ashtrays, filthy, look at all those butts, the place stinks like a tart's parlour.' She pointed a plain unvarnished finger at me; it looked like a sausage that had been caught in a steel shutter. 'Inspector Crowdie's waiting for you.'

'I'll just take my steroids and get over there, then,' I said.

'A dose of Ian Crowdie'll do you good,' she said.

'Oh, it's Ian already, is it?' said Stevenson lasciviously. 'How nice.'

'He was telling me in the canteen he's a keen rugby player,' said Andrewes. She turned red for some reason when she mentioned Cruddie, but that was book five chemistry that needed ideal conditions, not room 202 at eight in the morning. 'He's like a good whiff of the sea,' she said, 'you people make Soho smell like the South-East network, but he's like a brisk salty day.'

'Salt,' I said, 'I hate salt, it's the one thing I'm allergic to. I served down at Shorncliffe once – I don't like to think back.'

'Think forward then,' said Andrewes. 'The inspector's in 218, and waiting's a trick I don't think he's mastered.'

'He's a detective,' said Stevenson, 'he should have.'

'218,' I said, getting up, 'that's the end of the corridor where hell is.'

'And remember his rank when you get in there, won't you, dear?' Stevenson said to me, 'he'll likely be sensitive about that.'

'Rank's just symbolic,' I said.

Crowdie was sitting in 218 behind a battle-scarred metal table like my own, except that his was clean. When we had looked each other over he said: 'Sit down. They tell me we'll be working together, which from what I've heard sounds like hard work.'

'That's right,' I said, 'you'll find us funny folk at A14 – loners employed on clearing up unimportant deaths to close some little file, we don't come on like Chief Inspector Bowman over at Serious Crimes at all. We aren't allowed near anything that looks like page one, we've all been passed over for promotion, and we've all been punctured by buckshot, knives, or both.'

Crowdie got out a pack of crumpled filters, lit one and pushed them over to me.

'People keep telling you not to smoke,' he said. 'If they used the amount of television time they spend on smoking telling the public about the things we deal with in here they'd realise that we all might as well die of lung cancer, we're too disgusting to live.' He threw over some photographs of a dead girl.

I found myself taking to him. 'Yes,' I said, 'now there are people who see this face as net waste, a dead loss, but I see it as the face of someone who didn't want to go, or at any rate not like that. You get the people who say so what? She deserved it anyway, on the streets like that at fifteen, it's disgusting. In this city, anyway; I don't know about Dundee.'

'Never mind Dundee,' Cruddie said, 'we're a wearisome long way from it here, and talking of that I hear they call me Cruddie but my name's Crowdie and I was born on the

Clyde, so look out, I've a short fuse.'

'Cruddie's your nickname,' I said, 'you're lumbered with it now – mind you, you're doing well if you get a nickname here. Bowman hasn't a nickname.' I passed the morgue shots back and said: 'It would be nice to carry this discussion on another time – say over at The Trident. I don't know what brings you to Poland Street, I pity you, but maybe it's no ill wind.'

He said: 'Look down at Oxford Street in this fucking snow, and the folk hurrying about thinking they're making sense of the world when they're just using their wits while they can – and then one day they start getting bizarre feelings, one day when the rent's owing, and then they think fuck it and top themselves, or else go out and top some other poor bastard.'

'I don't know if what you're saying about people's the official view,' I said, 'it's certainly not the Factory's view. But it is my view. Killers don't care what they're doing – these people are insane for my money, I don't care what the judges say.'

'Forget the metaphysics,' Cruddie said, 'we're just here to catch them.'

'Don't I know it,' I said, 'but I wonder if you see my fury. A week back I had a mother whose fourteen-year-old daughter was raped on her way home from school – then the geezer cut her throat and I had to go and tell the mother that.'

'Scalp-warriors,' said Cruddie. 'They do it so as not to feel small, like kids dressing up to make the grown-ups take notice of them.'

'I do my best to look beyond our hateful ways,' I said. 'I only wish I had this country back the way it was. I don't care what was the matter with it, we were a fucking sight better off then than we are now.'

'Forget it,' said Cruddie, 'there was never any golden age.' He stood up. 'I hope we get on.'

'Looks as if we might,' I said, 'welcome to a small club.' We shook hands.

But that was before; that was Cruddie in the old days. Today he was much less co-operative. When I got in he said: 'Where the fuck have you been?'

'Over at Chalk Farm.'

'Well, drop it, whatever it is,' he said, 'there's a new lead on the Southall killing, they've asked us to check it out and everyone's tied up except you.'

'But I am tied up,' I said. I told him about Jidney.

'We've never even heard of this, how did you get on to it?'

'Firth. It started with his asking me to go up and see him for a chat.'

'Firth?' said Crowdie, 'he's just an old pisspot.'

'Firth had his eyes open,' I said, 'and he sent for me because I'm a mate of his. I've just been checking it out, and it's kosher.'

He said: 'But you say this Jidney's an old man?'

'Maybe,' I said, 'but that doesn't mean he's finished his life's work. He's got another woman lined up right now; Stevenson's watching her.'

'What?' said Crowdie. He exploded. 'You mean you told Stevenson to drop his work on your own initiative and sent him off on a case that doesn't even officially exist? What's the matter with you? Are you sick in your fucking mind or something?'

'All right,' I said, 'get Stevenson back, then, and we'll just sit here bleating about the rules all day while the Meredith woman gets killed. This Jidney's into her really hard, he's lined her up, and he's not the kind that likes being interrupted.'

'That's not the point,' said Crowdie, 'we work to a timetable here.'

'I know,' I said, 'but murder doesn't.'

'Well I've heard it all now, haven't I?' he said. 'I don't know why the rest of us don't just leave you to run the place one-handed.' He started coming on like Cryer. 'Have you got any evidence? Anything to go on at all?'

I told him how I had broken into Jidney's.

'Oh that does it,' said Crowdie, 'I've never heard anything like it – for sheer bottle, nothing like it! Well, you can forget your pension – you might as well clear your desk out and piss off home. Wait till Bowman hears about it, he'll do his pieces, he hates your guts.'

'I know he does,' I said, 'that's why I've come to see you.'

'You B and E this Jidney without a warrant, you've no body, you've got the square root of fuck-all, what else haven't you got?'

'I haven't got peace of mind over it,' I said.

'Look,' said Cruddie, 'I couldn't take you off Southall if I wanted to, I haven't the authority.'

'They don't need me over at Southall,' I said. 'You know that – you could send any experienced detective. Anyway, this Jidney thing, I'm not dropping it.'

'What the hell am I going to do?' said Cruddie.

'I don't know,' I said. 'Being an inspector brings terrible problems, it must be a nightmare.'

'See this ashtray here?' said Cruddie. 'Mind I don't clobber you with it.'

'All right,' I said, 'don't worry – I'll take it upstairs. I've done it before.'

'You're never going to Jollo with it,' said Cruddie in disbelief, 'that really proves you're mad.'

But I had already picked up the phone to talk to Jollo; instead, though, I found myself straight through to the Voice. I heard someone his end of the line say: 'Who's that on the phone?' and the Voice replying: 'The only man I know who thinks Placido Domingo's a bullfighter.' To me it said: 'Before you start I wanted to talk to you – how did you deal with the Harvist brothers? I forget.'

'The Harvists?' I said. 'Why bring that up? That's old history, this is about something brand new.'

'Never mind that,' said the Voice, 'just refresh my memory about the Harvists.'

I couldn't think why he was bothered about it. 'I went at it like an old woolly,' I said, 'just looked round till I found a loose strand called Gary and pulled on it. He was only a runner for them, but they trusted him with interesting messages.'

'You didn't go around arresting everyone in sight?'

'No, that was what Bowman wanted to do.'

'Never mind him. You pulled the man Gary in, didn't you?'

'That's right,' I said. 'Look, it's not the first of April, what's this about?'

'Just tell me what I want to know.'

'OK, there was just Stevenson and me – we put Gary under the lights and said: "Now you know how this works. An hour from now you'll have told us everything you know right down to next week's six easy draws." He said: "Will you arrest me when I've done that?" I said: "Of course not, Gary, don't be stupid." He said: "But I want you to arrest me." "I know you do," I said, "but I don't want you safe, I want it so that if you repeat what you're going to tell us to your folk they're going to hurt you, and if I find I'm not getting information from you it'll be me giving you a hard time."'

'There was some mess, wasn't there?'

'Not if you think of the one we cleared up.'

'Did Gary survive?'

'No sir. The Harvists decided he had to go so there was an accident with a truck, but that way we got the Harvists quietly instead of rushing about with warrants like teenyboppers with a credit card.'

'All right,' said the Voice, 'now what this is about, your name came up at a meeting.'

I knew what that meant. It meant the Voice had brought it up.

'And we discussed posting you away from A14. This endless battle of yours with DCI Bowman has got to stop.'

'I wouldn't agree to a transfer I'm afraid,' I said.

'Why not? You weren't with A14 for the Harvist case, but you handled it satisfactorily just the same.'

'Yes, we mopped them up,' I said. 'The Harvists are out of the nick now, doesn't time fly? I had a phone call from Johnny Harvist reminding me only the other day – friendly, I don't think.'

'Why does it matter to you, leaving A14?'

'It suits me here.'

'I wish it suited your colleagues.'

'It suits some of them. I agree there are the others.'

'So do I,' said the Voice. 'But this transfer, it's another department, you'd be co-ordinating operations. It would be a challenge with more pay, and it's dangerous.'

'All police work's dangerous,' I said, 'and I don't care about pay.'

'Christ!' said the Voice. It was the only violent word he ever used; he was said to be a mild-mannered man with a large family who lived near Basingstoke and went to church. 'This is to do with terrorists.'

'Terrorism is an armed lunatic in a bedsit to me.' I said, 'and always will be.'

'Terrorism is what I tell you it is,' said the Voice.

'See if this is terrorism,' I said. I told the Voice about Jidney, beginning with Carat Investments, then about breaking into Jidney's flat, right down to my having left Stevenson with Ann Meredith in her flat. I told it about the painting, the photograph album, the six-digit number and the cassette; I also told it about Jidney's fourteen years' form and the kind of offences he had gone down for.

'What was on this cassette? Have you run it through?'

'I haven't had a chance yet.'

The Voice said: 'There's enough crime waiting to be solved here without your finding more of it on your own – you're part of a team, we have our priorities, we have to tackle work according to the manpower available. Things have to go through channels, they have to wait.'

'Jidney doesn't know anything about channels,' I said, 'and this matter's very serious; it's sudden and it won't wait. It came to my attention through this conversation I had with Firth; I've checked it out and I've got to act on it.'

The Voice was silent, then it said: 'Now you listen to me. I take into consideration that sometimes I've made exceptions over the way you handle inquiries, and that sometimes I've roasted your balls off. What I'm telling you now is that the police isn't there simply to control a bunch of self-opinionated maniacs like you – at the moment it suffers from a very poor public image owing to cases of wrongful arrest and conviction, also of police corruption. All the press and the public are waiting for now is just one more balls-up, so might I just distract your attention from events at Thoroughgood Road and remind you that we have a general election coming up, and that a review of the police is high on the agenda. That means that if I get one dud result in the coming weeks my head's very likely to roll – and if it does, Sergeant, I shall create my own mayhem here, in which you will not be spared.' He added: 'As for Stevenson, you'd no right to send him off like that, and he'd no right to go.'

'I know,' I said. 'I also know I haven't got a body and Inspector Crowdie's upset about it. But what I am saying is that I'm putting myself on the line here – all I need is the assistance of one other officer, Sergeant Stevenson, and I guarantee I'll have Jidney parcelled up in three days. If I fall down over it I'll take the rap, but I've got to be taken off the Southall case.'

'I often think you'd be better off as a private detective.'

'No. I need the warrant card, it saves time.'

'You really think you and Stevenson can nail Jidney in three days?'

'All we've got to do is find him and bring him in before he kills anyone else.'

The Voice was silent for so long this time that I wondered if it had rung off, but in the end it said: 'All right, then, seventy-two hours.'

'I'll go over and tell Stevenson, then.'

'Yes, but keep me informed,' said the Voice, 'because if you drop me in the shit over this, I'll crucify you.' The phone went dead, and I left the building thinking about what used to happen to the early Christians when Nero got hold of them.

15

I went over to Maida Vale and told Stevenson everything. I explained exactly what I had got him into; then I produced Jidney's video. I said to Ann Meredith: 'Can we use your video machine here? Otherwise we'd have to get one in.' She looked as though she were about to sneer something like making yourselves at home, aren't you, but she was indignant instead.

'What do you want it for?'

'It's a video Sergeant Stevenson and I have got here,' I said. 'We'd probably better watch it just him and me together if that's OK.'

'Well, I can't very well say no, can I?' she said, 'but mind you don't ruin it, it's brand new. Though I must say, I really can't understand what you're both doing watching videos while I'm cooped up here.'

'If you'd just wait outside while we run it through.'

'It really is the limit!' she shouted. In the end we calmed her down and got her out; she stormed into her bedroom and slammed the door.

'She's not the easiest person to mind, is she?' I said to Stevenson.

'You've screwed up her love life,' said Stevenson, 'that's what she doesn't appreciate.'

I put the cassette into the machine. 'I don't know what we're going to see when we run this,' I said, sliding the cassette into the machine, 'but I think it's odds-on it's going to be nasty.'

'Well the machine won't flinch, whatever it is,' Stevenson said, 'it's Japanese.'

I pressed the play button and a small, bare area, brilliantly lit, appeared on the screen. The place was built of stone, with an arched ceiling, and it was damp; a narrow rhomboid box that served one purpose only projected from the foot of the frame. Against the far wall a naked woman with her feet towards us lay bound by her wrists and ankles; she was middle-aged, around fifty, and I knew her at once – her painted eyes had already stared past me in Jidney's place.

'Looks like a vault,' I said.

'I come from a family of gravediggers,' Stevenson muttered, 'and it is a vault. Who's the woman? Do you know her?'

'I know who she is,' I said. 'Or was.'

'Now, Flora,' said a naked man who had his back to us in a cajoling voice. 'Flora.'

The camera closed up to show her face – grey lips parted, eyes bright and terrified. They saw something we couldn't, they switched away from the camera and then she screamed.

'It's what we agreed, Flora,' said the man's voice. A noose of rabbit-wire dangled between her face and ours; it was fine wire and it caught the light. The woman started to speak, but she was so frightened that nothing she said made sense. The man made comforting noises several times trying to calm her down but gave up in the end and said savagely: 'Get where I want you, you cow!' She shook her head violently, but he was passing the noose round her neck anyway and pulled sharply. When the wire was deep into her neck he jerked it again; her face swelled and her cheeks reddened with congested blood, then darkened. The film went dark too.

When the screen brightened again we could see that things had been happening in the meantime; Flora didn't look intact any more. She had fatally changed, and other things about her had changed too. She was now badly cut across the breasts – they were open and half-severed by sweeping gashes which had left rivulets of blood wandering across her ribs. Her head lay sideways and looked wrong on her neck, yet her lips, thickened and purple, were still moving, trying to talk. There also was her aggressor. I could see it was Jidney now. His head was half-turned to the camera; he was squatting on her and spreading her legs apart; he had a huge erection which he exhibited to her, turning her head this way and that with his hand in her hair so as to force his penis into her mouth.

I stopped the film and turned to Stevenson. 'We'll have to watch all this somehow.'

'It's OK,' he said, 'my stomach's where it ought to be, just.' He broke off. 'Do you hear something, it was the bedroom door opening, wasn't it? For Christ's sake let's not have any interruptions, wait a minute.' He went to the door and called out: 'Miss Meredith? Are you all right?'

'Of course I'm all right,' she shouted back impatiently from the corridor. 'What are you doing in there? Are you going to stay in there all afternoon watching movies?'

Stevenson said calmly: 'Just wait where you are for now, we'll be out in a minute. Don't come in here till we tell you, that's all.'

'Why not?' she shouted through the door. 'What are you watching?' When we didn't answer she said: 'Is it anything to do with Henry?'

Stevenson just said: 'We really won't be long now, Miss Meredith.'

I shut the door, spotted a key in the lock and turned it. 'All right,' I said, 'let's get on with it.'

I restarted the machine. Jidney was on top of Flora on the stone floor now, with the rabbit-wire round her neck.

Her eyes were popping out of her head and glazed; she was barely alive. He was penetrating her, biting her simultaneously in the breasts and they were both screaming, Jidney with his mouth full of blood. Then he pulled the wire so tightly that her neck, leaving nothing but a dark crease where the noose vanished, looked like a child's balloon at the nozzle end where you tie the string. 'Not so fast, not so fucking fast, you bitch!' he gurgled, enraged, and she died as he came, flopping in just one spasm; when it was over he rolled off her, then turned back on his hands and knees and began to play with her body, making noises. All at once he dropped her, and whirled round at the camera from his squatting position. 'Why don't you move any more?' he screamed. His lips lay back in a snarl along his teeth, spit flew off his bottom lip: 'Why don't you fucking move?' The woman's body shuddered in his grip. He turned to an airline bag beside him on the floor and took an eighteen-inch knife out of it. He lined the knife up along the crease the wire made in her neck and cut; in four strokes the head was off. He took the head by the hair and held it up to the camera; then there was no more film.

Stevenson said nothing for a while. He had turned a bad colour, pearl shading off to green round his mouth. After swallowing a few times he muttered: 'All right, let's just talk, have you any idea how many he's done?'

'It could be as many as sixteen,' I said. 'Or more even, I don't know.'

'We've got to find Jidney,' said Stevenson. 'That vault, the bodies. What are you going to do?'

'I'm taking this to Jollo now,' I said, rewinding the cassette.

'What about Meredith? I can't watch her round the clock single-handed.'

'I know you can't,' I said, 'she'll have to be moved.'

I called her in. 'Well?' she said. 'What did you see on the film? I imagine I've the right to know.'

Instead of answering her I said: 'Would you mind going upstairs with Sergeant Stevenson and packing everything you think you might need for a few days?'

'What?' she said. 'Where am I going? Isn't it all right if I just stay here and don't let anyone in?'

'No,' I said, 'I'm afraid not.'

She blew up. 'You don't mean to say I'm under arrest on top of everything else?'

'Of course not. We're taking you into custody for your own protection.'

'What are you talking about? I know I only work part-time, but what about my job? What are my employers going to say?'

'We'll explain to your employers.'

'Where are you taking me?'

'To a safe house,' I said, 'but it'll take time to arrange, meanwhile you'll have to stay in a police station, probably Poland Street, I don't know yet.'

She said: 'I don't understand what's happening, I still don't believe any of it.'

All Stevenson said to her politely was: 'I'll help you pack.'

16

Firth rang in and said: 'Jidney's left here in his motor – just himself and an airline bag.'

I held Firth while I rang Stevenson to tell him that, but I wasn't too worried about the bag, not with Stevenson at Maida Vale. 'He'll get short shrift at Meredith's and he'll be back,' I said when I got back to Firth.

'How can you be so sure?'

'He's got no choice,' I said. 'Put yourself in his place. He doesn't know what to do. Of course he wants to abandon Thoroughgood Road, but he can't. He's got to stick to it like shit to a blanket, because my bet is that he's left gear in there and he's got to move it.'

'What sort of gear?'

'Gear that probably smells,' I said, 'after that video and the painting I wouldn't put anything past him. Could even be bits of people – the first thing I noticed when I searched the place was that the windows were open top and bottom, though it was a freezing cold day. I didn't notice any smell, but that doesn't mean there aren't things well past their sell-by date hidden there somewhere; I hadn't time to take the pad apart the way I'm going to the next time I go round. That's part one of his nightmare; part two is that not only does the cassette show him in the process of committing a murder; it also reveals the vault, and if anybody finds that vault he's cooked. Then there's the rest of the scenario. Ronald's got to move these items in case whoever whizzed the video goes in for a second bite and finds them – yet at the same time he's scared he's being watched and likely to be stopped on his way out with the gear on him. The one thing that's sure by now is that he knows his cassette's gone, and as long as he's not tracked that down he'll be flying round and round the neighbourhood like a bat at a bonfire wondering who the thief was and, worse still, how the hell he was rumbled.'

'Do you reckon he thinks it was the law that took the cassette?'

'How can he know we're onto him,' I said, 'and yet how can he know we're not? He thought he was a hundred per cent hidden and that's the point – he must be tearing his hair out wondering how the hell anyone got onto him – even if he thought it was you he wouldn't connect you with us in a thousand years. And then, on the other hand, if it isn't the law, he must be beating his brains out wondering who the hell it could have been, how, and why. Carat's the only possibility, he'll think, but there'll be no blip from there – one wrong move from Darko and he's an accessory to murder, ten to fifteen years with his form; I told him and he freaked.'

'Then there's Meredith,' said Firth. 'It must have shaken the shit out of him when he heard her talking to us in my room, because you can bet that was him at the window – and now he'll be wondering where the hell she's gone and why she isn't answering her 'phone at Maida Vale.'

'Well, you saw him leave here with that airline bag,' I said, 'and thank God Stevenson's with her, but I shan't be happy till she's in a police station or in a safe house – not after what I saw happen to Flora.' I swallowed because I felt sick at the memory. 'Finding death isn't the same as watching it happen.'

'It was really that bad?'

'If you'd seen it you wouldn't need to ask.'

'Even so, I don't see how you can nail Jidney yet – you still haven't got a body.'

'Not that you could do an autopsy on, no,' I said, 'but that cassette will get any jury running for the jacks, and as likely as not the judge too.'

'This cassette. Is Jidney in it?'

'In it?' I said. 'He made it. He set the camera running and he's the star – I'll need you to identify him when the time comes. The victim too.'

'I've seen death often enough,' said Firth, 'but I don't think I ever want to see that film.'

'You'll be called as a witness when this goes to trial,' I said, 'so I'm afraid you may have to. Meanwhile I'd rather not talk about it.'

'Do you think he's got many more videos like that?'

'Who knows?' I said, 'but this one will do.'

'You've still got a lot of miles to do.'

'I know I have,' I said. 'Miles into hell, and I'm afraid.'

17

I rang Frank Ballard because I had to; I felt the overpowering need to lean on a friend's reason. 'I feel physically sick, Frank,' I said when he answered, 'I need help, advice, a friend, and have you got a video player? I've got something I need you to see on it, I'm afraid.'

'Afraid?'

'Right now I'm afraid of my shadow.'

When I got round I told him I was in trouble with a case and added: 'I've been making enemies at work again. Bowman.'

'People like you hit a brick wall just as hard as other people,' said Ballard. 'I can't seem to get it into your head that you might as well go round punching donkeys in Galway as have a go at men like Bowman.'

Frank had moved into a ground-floor flat over at Kensal Rise; it had a long sitting-room and french windows leading into a tangled garden. I ought to explain about Frank. He was a first-rate detective who transferred to A14 for the same reasons I did, cutting himself off from the career he deserved with the high-fliers over at Serious Crimes.

But a career of any kind finished for him, anyway, the summer night in 1980 when he was off duty and driving home down Fulham Palace Road; there he saw a cook on his own in a take-away being menaced by a villain in a balaclava with a sawn-off. Frank stopped and sprinted in there, telling the thief to put the gun down, but as he turned to tell the cook to get down on the floor the thief fired, hitting Frank in the spine; then he ran off and we never got him, though it's a file that'll never be closed. Frank was paralysed from the waist down; they told him his spinal cord would grow at a rate of one millimetre a year and he wanted to die at first, even though he had been decorated and the Queen Mother came to see him in hospital; but instead of despairing he took an honours degree in philosophy and psychology through Open University and he's a PhD now, costs you a dollar to speak to him, and I go to him whenever I'm in difficulty just as I always used to, which is what friends are for. He follows what we're all doing in the papers or on television or else we go and see him; his brain's better than it ever was, and as he says himself, he's got nothing to do but sit and think anyway, so he might as well make the most of it.

'I'm resigned now,' he told me once, 'and that's good. Better than being dragged off kicking and screaming.'

I wonder if he really meant that deep down; but anyway, now he gets around really fast in what he calls his electric chair, and it's not often I come up with a problem and he hasn't some new slant to offer.

'How about a beer?' he said when I got there, but he had already gone to get us one. 'All right,' he said when we were ready, 'who's the body?'

'There isn't one yet,' I said, 'that's the trouble – all I've got is one waiting to happen.'

'Then how do you know you've got a killer on your hands at all?'

'Because he makes high-grade murder movies.' I told him all I knew about the Jidney business so far, then produced the cassette. 'This man's writer, cameraman, producer, director and central character in a cast of two,' I said. I switched on the video recorder. 'I wouldn't normally bother to say this to you, Frank,' I said, 'but this is a film you want to take very easy – we don't have to watch it all at once, we can do it in stages.'

'I hope I haven't gone that soft,' he said.

I shook my head. 'This is different. You've got the soundtrack and all. Stevenson and I have just seen it.'

So then we watched it through; we managed to do it in one. Being the second time for me, and what with the soundtrack, I think it was worse for me than for Frank. When it was over Ballard said: 'How did you get onto this?'

'Firth used his brains,' I said, 'and to think I didn't take him seriously to start with.'

'I take it back about the movie,' said Ballard, 'my nerves must be going back on me, there were a couple of times there when I thought I was going to spew.'

'You aren't the only one,' I said. 'You ought to see the painting the man does too – he's a real fucking artist, some collector freak would pay him a fortune. He's got to be put in the shade, Frank – in fact if I had my way he'd leave the building for good. But it's teasing. Here I've got the body, and I've got the killer, there they both are on film, but they're only on film. I even know where he lives, thanks to Firth, only Ronnie won't do me the favour of being in when I call so I can't have a word with him, what a shame. So one of the things I've got to find out, before his next women gets done, is where this was shot and the name of the woman in it. But the trying thing is that I've only got seventy-two hours, otherwise I'm in schtuck with the Voice, and that's another problem.'

'Why don't you just get the Voice to see that video,' said Ballard. 'You'd get more time.'

'I can't,' I said, 'the Voice is in Paris on an EC police conference. George Jollo's in charge.'

'Oh Christ,' said Ballard, 'getting him to see anything is like teaching the alphabet to a brick wall.'

'Yes,' I said, 'but luckily I've got Stevenson on loan in spite of Bowman trying to get him off me, so I'd rather the two of us tried to crack it in the time.'

'You got any name for this runner of yours besides Ronnie?'

'I've got several,' I said, 'but I don't know whether I've got them all. The name he goes under in the house he lives in, which is where Firth lives, is Henry Cross. On the other hand he owns four houses run through a property company, Carat Investments, managed by a little deviator called Freddy Darko, where he appears as a man called Rich. But Barry's dug me up a file for the same face under the name of Jidney, Ronald James, whereas his current girlfriend is convinced he's a Mr Drury. You ever heard of anyone called Jidney, Frank? Does he ring a bell with you?'

He shook his head.

'Well there you are,' I said, 'that's you, me and Firth, we none of us make him, and yet look at his sheet here, look at the form he's got.'

Frank looked at it, but he could only say the same as Firth had – no one could keep up from memory with every villain we had on the books. 'And you've no idea who the victim in the film is?'

'Barry's been checking her on Missing Persons,' I said, 'and there's a chance it could be Flora Borthwick, fifty-four, unmarried. The dates fit, only the face Barry's got of her is just from a holiday snap, and the resolution's so bad and shows her as so much younger that he can't be sure.'

'Well, we can make a guess where he got the houses from,' said Ballard, 'You'll have to check the past owners back through the land registry.'

'That's what Firth said, and of course we will, but it'll take too long; I want Jidney now, before he kills anyone else. This new woman Meredith he's got on the hook, for instance.'

'Anyone else missing apart from Flora?'

'It could be half the women's army corps for all I know,' I said, 'but if each of the photographs in the album I found is a death, then it could be sixteen to be going on with.'

'Jesus Christ.'

Together we went over everything I had copied down in Jidney's flat. When I came to the six-digit figure I said: 'I picked this up – it might have everything to do with the case or nothing at all, I don't know because I can't make head or tail of it. Which is sod's law, Frank, because if it is a lead it's about the only one I've got.'

He looked at it for a while and then said: 'Can't you make anything of it?'

'Do you mean you can?'

'I'm not sure,' he said, 'but it mentions here on his file that your Ronnie did his national service.'

'So what of it?'

'It's just an idea.' He moved over to a row of bookshelves at the end of the room, picking up a long pole with a hook on the way. He looked up at a line of tall volumes on the top shelf and muttered: 'This is the tricky part – try catching this as it comes down, but mind your head.' He got the hook into the top of one of the books and pulled on it until it toppled and fell into my arms.

He motored over to a big table and opened the book on it. He had Jidney's six-figure number beside him and started leafing through the pages of the book; looking over his shoulder I saw it was a volume of Ordnance Survey maps.

'Did you find any maps like these in his pad when you turned it over?'

I said no.

'Never mind,' he said, 'here we are, let's see what we've got.' He was looking at a section of Kent countryside, halfway between Maidstone and Tonbridge. He put his finger on a wild-looking bit, murmuring: 'Happens to be a part of the world I know, we used to picnic round there when I was a kid. We used to come down from London at weekends. Of course it was all real countryside in those days, though even now this bit doesn't look much altered.' He had his finger over a dense stretch of woodland. 'Well,' he said, 'at least it makes sense.'

'What does?'

'Well, you can see that this is a map reference and that my finger's on a church, can't you?' he said impatiently. 'Here, have a look – this is it, off the M25. Here's Sevenoaks over here, here's Westerham, and now we're out on the Edenbridge Road. Now here's your church, and where you've a church you're likely to have a vault. Lots of vaults. And my bet is that one of them is where he does all of them.' He pushed the map across. 'I don't know what you could expect to find when you go down there, but I daresay he likes revisiting his old girlfriends – the shrinks call it the totem stage, going down to sit looking at the ivy, musing over old times, even digging a few of them over in sunny weather, having a wank – you know the funny kind of fun these funny people have.'

18

I rang the Factory from Ballard's place and got through to Detective Chief Superintendent George Jollo. Due to old history, a matter of my being reinstated after my suspension at the end of a case in spite of his direct opposition, Jollo and I had never got on.

'All right,' he said when I arrived in his room, 'I know about this crack-brained thing you're on. And by the way, we've got a terrible woman here called Meredith making an uproar, is that anything to do with you?'

'It certainly is,' I said. 'Now wake your ideas up and adjust your attitude, George, because her life's in danger from a man connected to a Kent churchyard where at least one woman, and I've good reason to think a great many more, has died violently, by which I mean murdered.'

'First things first!' he shouted. 'That can wait, I've also got DCI Bowman doing his nut over you.'

'There's no time to worry about him,' I said, 'and for Christ's sake will you just forget the rule-book and take this seriously. If you think bringing Ann Meredith here is just a fuss about nothing, wait till you see a home movie I've got with me here – you'll ruin your shirt-front.' I threw the cassette on his desk.

He said: 'Where did that come from?'

'I broke into a man's flat and nicked it,' I said.

He threw his head back and laughed. 'If I really thought

you meant that,' he said, 'I'd bust you on the spot.'

'I'll tell you the truth then, George,' I said mildly, 'a fairy dropped it on her way overhead.'

'All right, then,' he said, 'what's in the fucking thing, anyway?'

'Let's go down to Records where they've got a video player and have a look,' I said, 'but I warn you the material it contains is horrific.' Barry got us a video player and I put the cassette in, saying to Jollo: 'I'm not too sure if I can watch this again, but I'll try.' When it was over I turned to Jollo; I thought he was going to faint.

'First time round for you with snuff?' I asked him.

'No,' he said. He was like a different man. 'But it's the first time I've ever seen anything like this before, even at Poland Street.'

'There are no words for it, are there?' I said.

'No,' said Jollo. 'All right, what do you need?'

'I want a warrant for Ronald James Jidney, and an unmarked car in Thoroughgood Road with an intelligent crew in it. I shall have to take Stevenson with me into the house to make the arrest because Firth can't – he's no longer a police officer.'

'Can you identify Jidney?'

'We all can. I passed him on the stairs at Thoroughgood Road. Firth's his neighbour. Meredith's his girlfriend, and Records has got him on the books anyway.'

'Are you going to show this film to the girlfriend?'

'Of course not,' I said. 'It would destroy her, and what good would that do? All it would prove to her is that Jidney really is a monster, and that will come out at his trial anyway, if he's fit to plead. But what I am going to do when I bring Jidney in is to play it in front of him and in front of us and in front of his solicitor, and see if we can get him to make a statement.'

'What are we going to do about Meredith?'

'Keep her here until we've got Jidney, that's vital – we

can't leave her unguarded while he's running about. He must realise we're after him by now as it is, but when he finds she's left home as well he's going to go fucking potty.'

'I understand all right,' said Jollo, 'only I've got Chief Inspector Bowman screaming for men.'

'He's always screaming for men,' I said, 'he sends for the Flying Squad if some kid nicks a chocolate bar in a supermarket.'

'I'll do what I can.'

'Mind you do,' I said, 'because I'm in the business of saving life, not taking chances, and if Jidney thinks he's got a chance he'll be in there, and we've already got sixteen examples of what'll happen then. But Meredith's obstinate; she's convinced she's in love with this maniac and she hates being immobilised, but you'll have to make her see sense. Anyway, catching Jidney shouldn't take long – and meanwhile find that vault in Kent, you've got the map reference. Turn it right over when you get there – you might even find Jidney inside. But I'm going to wait for him at home.'

'A vault,' said Jollo, 'of all places.'

'It's not stupid,' I said, 'that's why he's been killing scot-free for years. It's only forty-four miles from London, isolated, room for the video, sound-proof, the victim can scream her head off and no one to hear, it's perfect.'

'Well, vandalising graves is all the rage nowadays,' said Jollo, 'this is just the new twist. Burke and Hare must be going mad wherever they are, they took out the patent.'

When the warrant arrived I got up and Jollo saw me to the door. 'I've tried, but I've never liked you, Sergeant,' he said. 'What's the use?'

'You haven't tried hard enough, George,' I said, putting the warrant away, 'the secret's the same as with detective work, you've got to keep at it.'

19

I had to wait most of the afternoon while they got their car organised (the first one had a blue lamp on top and said 'Police' down the side) so I used the time for a final check on Ann Meredith, because I had long ago learned at Poland Street never to leave anything to run itself. It was a place like a government where you could never get hold of the people you really needed, whereas there were far too many people pounding up and down that you hadn't ordered, and the more there were of those the likelier it was that some enthusiast with a bit of authority and not enough to do would make a balls-up of something or other if he got a chance.

I rang Jollo's extension but it didn't answer, so I got the desk to put me through to whoever was in the charge of his office. I waited. The longer I waited the less I liked it; it was the kind of silence that was police code for a cock-up, and a hollow feeling fell through my stomach and ended in my feet.

Finally a voice said: 'Davidson.'

He was a DC I hardly knew. 'Where's Mr Jollo?' I said.

'He's sitting in on an interrogation. Can I help you?'

'I hope so,' I said. 'Give me an update on Ann Meredith and set my mind at rest.'

'Meredith, Meredith . . .'

'Ann Meredith is a witness and probable next target of

a multiple killer,' I said. 'She's somewhere in this building in the charge of Mr Jollo, and I'm ringing to check she's where she's supposed to be.'

'Hold on while I find out.'

He put the phone down; over the line I heard people moving about, the clatter of a tray; someone said something which ended with the words 'a load of bollocks', and there was some easy-going laughter.

When Davidson came back on the air again he said: 'I'm sorry, but the surveillance on Ann Meredith has been taken off.'

Whatever I had been prepared for, it wasn't that. I turned cold and said very slowly: 'Would you just repeat that?'

He did so and added: 'They said they hadn't the men.' He seemed to realise I wasn't happy about it; I sensed him wincing over the phone.

'Who gave the order?' I said.

'That I couldn't tell you.' He added: 'I can assure you it didn't come from this office.'

'Then you can count on still being alive tomorrow,' I said, 'but the berk responsible for this fuck-up won't be so lucky.'

I knew she wouldn't be there, but I dialled Meredith's home number for the sake of something to do while I pulled myself together. I knew what the answer would be – no answer – and I was not only right but, far worse, the number was unobtainable. The lump in my stomach now turned to lead; I redialled Poland Street and asked for Jollo again. This time I got him, asked him about Meredith, and when I had the same answer as I'd had from Davidson I kept my voice down somehow and said: 'Before we go any further, has this got anything to do with Charlie Bowman?'

When he didn't say no I said: 'Wait till I get hold of that salaried murderer, but don't let's bother with that now.

Have you tried ringing Meredith? Well, do it and ring me back, I'm downstairs in 202.'

When he rang back I said: 'Did you get the same answer as I did, unobtainable? Yes? Well someone had better get to that flat faster than five minutes ago, and if there's been a death over there I can tell you that whoever's responsible for it is going to get killed over here.'

'DCI Bowman takes precedence over you, Sergeant,' said Jollo, 'that's what rank means.'

'If he's responsible for turning sixteen deaths into seventeen,' I said, 'he'll be working out what rank means on his way to the cemetery.'

'He decided to take Stevenson off Meredith and let her go home, which was what Meredith wanted anyway.'

I didn't bother to answer that. 'Where is Stevenson now, anyway?'

'Over at Southall,' said Jollo, 'I hate to say I told you so.'

For the first time in my life I actually tried to pull some of my hair out. 'You mean Bowman's put him on another case?' I said. 'But Meredith was top priority – I'd got clearance right the way down from the Voice, and you know it.'

'Just a minute,' said Jollo, 'I've got a call on the other line.' He came back to me and said in a low voice: 'I've got an officer here who'd like a word with you, I'll put you through.'

It was a police patrol car driver. He sounded shaken. 'We received a call from the neighbours of this Miss Meredith over here at Maida Vale – we couldn't get an answer ringing the bell so we broke in.'

'And she's dead,' I said.

'It's worse than just that,' he said, 'it's terrible, worst I've ever seen. You'd better come over.'

The street door of Ann Meredith's block of flats was wide open, and there was a squad car outside. I saw the sergeant in charge and identified myself. In the hallway downstairs a middle-aged woman in a flowered dressing-gown was being comforted by a policewoman; when she turned to me I saw there was a big bruise on her cheekbone, fresh.

'All right,' I said, 'what happened?'

The WPC said to the witness: 'I know it's painful, but could you manage to repeat to this officer what you told us?'

It didn't take long. The witness had heard a series of screams from Meredith's flat and had come down to see what was going on – she wondered if she had perhaps hurt herself or anyway had some kind of accident. She had seen no one come into the house, yet as she arrived at Meredith's door it was wrenched open, and a man in dark clothes wearing a black woollen cap and carrying an iron bar had torn out, clobbered her and run out into the street, turning left at the corner, she thought. She wasn't sure, she had her hands up to her face. Immediately afterwards she had heard a car starting – she hadn't got a sight of the car, of course.

'All right,' I told her, 'get some rest till the ambulance comes, you're lucky to be alive.' I said to the sergeant: 'You're the scene of crime officer. Have you been into the flat yet?'

'I'm going in now.'

'I'd like to come with you.'

'All right. If you don't disturb anything.'

Inside, Meredith's flat was dark and the blinds were drawn. In a corner the phone had been ripped out of the wall and thrown across the room; in another corner lay what looked like a bundle of dirty clothes. The bundle of clothes looked surprisingly small for a body, but that was because it was lying with its knees up in its stomach and had its face, partly covered with a blanket, turned to the wall. I went and knelt down by Meredith; I moved the blanket slightly with the sergeant's permission and found that the head was nearly off, the neck cut through to the spinal column by the strokes of a knife. The violence was so recent that its aura was still as loud in the room as a last sharp word, together with the iron smell of blood. There was blood all over the walls and floor, too, and the blouse which the killer had ripped off the dead woman and thrown into a corner on top of the ripped-out telephone was sodden with it. There was a frenzy in this murder even more marked than in the other I had seen on the cassette – evidence of a helter-skelter fury in the way the body had been violated and objects hurled and scattered everywhere, as though the perpetrator sensed that we were within reaching distance of him and had succumbed to his rage and terror, his hatred bursting his disguises of outward normality, his assumed nice-guy personality exploding together with Ann Meredith's life.

I took Meredith's head in my hands and turned it gently towards me. My hands were immediately covered with blood; the sight reminded me of my dream about the dead man outside the town of Jer. She had no face left to speak of; nothing remained but a red pulp with moist blue-white splinters of bone – nose, jaw, forehead – projecting from it. Now I also noticed how the black skirt she wore had been hauled up round her waist, and that something was protruding from her behind. This object was also bloody and there was a smear of drying semen at my end; I saw it to be the snapped off part of a broom-handle.

'You were angry with her, weren't you, Ron?' I whispered as I looked down at her. 'You weren't going to have her getting away from you, were you, so you went and topped her and made her number seventeen, because I have started to seriously fuck you about and you don't like it, do you?' As I put her head down again carefully, there was a horrible soft feeling about it as it touched the floor.

The scene of crime officer came out of the bedroom. He pointed behind him and said: 'She was sexually assaulted in here. There's sperm all over the bottom sheet.' I joined him and leaned over the shambles of the bed, staring at what Italians call the little map of love.

'He didn't half get his rocks off when he did come, the old darling,' said the officer.

'I've got to catch him,' I said, 'and do it fast; he's completely unstable now, out of control. He's angry and upset. He's had to abandon his precious routine. He's let his temper get on top of him, he's killed in haste because he was thwarted; he didn't get his ritual, couldn't take her to the vault, nothing – he's all unsatisfied, well choked.'

'Then he'll make more mistakes from now on, with a bit of luck.'

'But they won't bring Ann Meredith back,' I said, and I felt bad at having thought of her as an obstinate, irritating person – at ever having been so petty.

20

I was standing with Stevenson a hundred yards down the street from twenty-three Thoroughgood Road.

Stevenson said: 'Are you going straight up there?'

'Yes,' I said, 'I'm going to sit there and wait for him. If he's picked up down in Kent or anywhere else let me know – but my bet is he'll come here, because there are items upstairs he hasn't collected that he can't afford to let us find.'

Firth joined us. 'You need me up in that room? You'd better have back-up.'

'No,' I said. 'Just the shock that my being there will give Jidney, that'll be back-up enough.'

'You armed?'

'I never go armed,' I said. 'I only ever went armed once in my life, and that was for Tony Spavento.'

'You could wait a long time for Jidney,' Firth said.

'I tell you he's got stuff up there that he's got to move,' I said, standing up, 'and he hasn't much time to do it in. But I've got all my time.'

Upstairs I sat in the dark, in Jidney's armchair in his sitting-room with my back to the window, facing the door. I sat there, completely still, wondering, not what was going to happen now, but how it would happen, and how soon, my tongue like a ball of fluff that had smouldered out in my mouth, and I picked at a crust made by fear at the corner of my lips.

When would it happen? When would he come? In a minute, an hour? I had the floorboards up, all ready, and the six tins with the souvenirs laid out on the joists for us to have a chat over, just the two of us together. I could have had Stevenson arrest him in the street, and by the book I should have, or I could have had Stevenson in the room with me and should have, but I didn't want that; I wanted just Ron and me to be together. So I left Stevenson down in the street with the others and had arranged for them to come up if I switched a light on, or to kick the door in if they heard anything loud going wrong, such as a gun being fired.

Jidney had to come in and try to get his souvenirs. Over the last decades he had got lazy, perhaps even indifferent to discovery, believing, as most of those people did, that the high jump could never happen to him; he could easily have stopped thinking about that possibility. But as for me, I sat there with my immediate and unknowable future going round and round in my head – how it would happen, and what my fate would be wearing when it entered, what Jidney might have in his hand when he came through the door. I looked at my watch; it said five past seven. It could have said five past eternity and I wouldn't have noticed; the cheap dial looked white as a frightened face on my arm when I held it to the street light to watch the quartz-driven second hand drifting coldly past the numerals, leaving time behind.

Nothing in the room moved; the whole world was silent except where far off, too far for me, on a different planet, a police car's siren screamed on the trail of a different errand with a noise like the devil's joy.

I was afraid. I knew, I had often been told, that fear evaporated when you faced it, and I just hoped the people who had told me that were right. The way I live you always think you've considered death from every possible angle, but when your number crops up it always turns out that you never have.

This fear I had now wouldn't go away because it was part of me; I felt it would only leave when I took it by the hand and left with it. But how can you be separated from what you're a part of? This must be what the dying feel, when mind and body are together, and for the first time so far off. I would have given anything to have Ballard, Stevenson, Cruddie with me now. But all I had was the buttons of Jidney's brown armchair cushions sticking into me as I forced myself just to listen and sit still.

Cold blood, cold turkey; now that I was in it I would rather have died suddenly, in a fight, than have this contest come up on me silently, on its own patch, at an unknown hour; even though I had wanted it, now that it was nearly on top of me I found I didn't want it at all. So I passed the time trying, too late, to get to know my soul and draw comfort from my dead, from Dahlia, from my father.

My father said that the hardest thing in life was the first thing – to think of others in a world that taught you to think of yourself. But he said it was worth it, and now I believed I knew what he meant all right – that if you didn't understand people you didn't exist. I was paid to catch people who didn't exist; the people whose shoulders I tapped left only the dead behind them.

Now memories of my father fled past me and I tried to catch them. He had been a clerk in a South London drapery store and had volunteered, over-age, to defuse mines; but our last talk had been in the hospital. A nurse with a stiff face and a healthy body rustling inside her starch came with morphine for him, trying not to show she prayed, and my father, swollen but propped up and comfortably trapped in bed with the cancer in his groin told me at last how it had been on the commando training course in Scotland in '41, and how he had come back to my mother with his lieutenant's pips up before he had gone down to North Africa to clear up the German mines, striding through the door and dumping his cap and holdall by the gas fire at our two-up, two-down in Lewisham to say, tanned-looking and surprised: 'Well, it's a change from selling knickers in SE12 – first and last commissioned officer you'll find in this family.' He gasped with laughter at the white walls as he told me this, rattling on about his first night's leave; he also told me that was the night my sister Julie was conceived.

He also told me for the first time that the morning it was his turn to get down to the beach to tackle a real mine it wasn't like the classroom any more at all where he had been prepared with fifteen other young men wearing cadets' white tapes, notepads placed exactly in front of them on the desks of the requisitioned grammar school, listening gravely to a mining engineer turned colonel as he explained percussion caps, detonators and the required strength of charges, the exact lengths of wire and the strength of batteries the enemy used. Reality was nothing after the first reality, my father said; reality was the first mine you tackled, and if you survived that first reality it never really came back, much as a multiple murderer's real pleasure is only his first. My father said that reality never returned if you already knew what to do about it and knew more or less how it was going to be, because the novelty and terror of death, the blinding explosion, like first love, had already come and gone.

He told me he had surprised himself. He had not known he could do it, tackling these objects that were as cold and passive as himself. The people from the War Office sat perched on shooting-sticks at a safe distance under the dunes while the sea roared greyly in and the Guards major stared down the shore at him through his binoculars and wrote things on a clipboard; and he had come through the whole war without a scratch to die, not blown to bits by any exterior device, but demolished from inside his own body by a melanoma, which had begun as a black stain on his back and followed him to his groin where it burst through his thigh – finally nothing more alien than his own flesh had undone him.

I too, in my own way, was a defuser of mines, and now it was my turn to be alone, sitting in a chair above a different form of death that I was constructed to find and beat; I was in terror's own front room, my performance no doubt being noted on a different form of clipboard whose observations could not save me if anything went wrong; I felt a pen scratching my judgment in a different part of my head where the text-book logic of my brain and the silence of the room were. Now it was my turn to sit in death's own chair that offered me its worn arms beside the gaping floorboards which had hidden flesh turned to vaguely smelling filth by the man I was waiting for. I thought, well, come soon, even if as a result I'm just absent and so no longer obliged to care; at worst, the great load will have gone, the cup swallowed and removed, the deal over.

I reflected about not having courage, but being driven by conviction – that was why I always thought of the example set me by Ballard, and the reason why I was thinking of him now.

I also thought that, being everywhere and nowhere, somehow you ended up being everywhere, seeing everything. It sounds stupid to say so, but I think that if there were such a thing as previous existence I must be purging some very heavy charge to the past to be doing this kind of work, to know I shall go on doing it, and to have had the grief I've had in my private life to go with it.

All I had to do was wait. I had opened Jidney's tins of relics, examined them as my father would have examined the interior of a mine and closed them again; now I had them all laid out along the edges of the floorboards I had raised.

When I heard Jidney come upstairs and put his key into the lock and turn it, when I saw him come in I looked up at him and said quietly: 'Hullo.'

He said: 'What are you doing here?'

I said: 'You are Ronald Jidney.'

He said: 'What is it to you?'

I cautioned him and said: 'I am a police officer. I have a warrant, and I am arresting you on a charge of murder.'

He said: 'I refuse to answer. I know nothing about any murder.'

I said: 'Do you know nothing about these tins laid out here?'

He said: 'I have never seen them before.'

I said: 'You will have to do better than that.'

He said: 'What will I have to do?'

I said: 'You will have to open these tins over here where the floorboards are up, the tins in front of me. I have done so, and know what they contain.'

He said: 'You know I cannot do that.'

I said: 'Then you had better come with me and we will continue this conversation at Poland Street police station.'

He said: 'Thank God it is over. Do you hate me?'

'No,' I said. 'You will never realise the horror of what you have done.'

'I don't know what you mean.'

I said: 'Look, seeing what you've done, if I were to hit you very hard, for instance, do you think that would be a good thing?'

'Oh that!' he said. 'You don't mean good, do you, you mean violence. Oh that's all right, I know all about that.'

He quite obviously had no idea what I was talking about so I said: 'We had better just go downstairs now.'

He agreed at once and we walked down to the street where Stevenson was waiting; Firth was with him. I thanked Firth for everything he had done and said: 'Well, the end of a case is like any other kind of future, I suppose, it takes a long time to arrive, but it gets there in the end, like British Rail. Which car?'

'The first one.'

'Then let's put him on board.'

Now that it was over, what I had found under Jidney's floorboards had time to catch up with me and at last I could be sick, which I was, untidily, in the gutter. Far back, the night that woman threw the knife at me in South London and I got it in the stomach and was sure I was dying, something went through my head that I never afterwards forgot: that I was in a large low room and there were a lot of people in there; whether I knew them or not I still knew them. From there we all moved out through a french door into a garden on a summer evening; it was full of trees with fruit hanging from the branches, and there were peaches and apricots pruned and trained up red brick walls – it was a cool, quiet place where we had all long desired to be. Then, after we had been there for a while, we all moved off of our own accord without saying a word into the country beyond whose horizon was unending and white, discussing the coming encounter with the people we knew we were to meet. We had a long discussion on the way which was peaceful, because all the tired old questions were over now; everything was over and the verdict on every one of us was in – no matter who we were, or thought we had been, or had somehow been persuaded that we were.

Jidney said again: 'Thank God it is over,' as we got into the car. We all got in with him without any fuss and drove off, and that was all there was to it.

Not till after the news of the arrest had broken in the press, in fact the next day, did I speak to a man who had at last come forward to tell us he had known Ron when they had worked together on a building-site thirty years ago. 'He seemed a very ordinary bloke to me and the rest of the lads,' he said, 'very quiet man. Although –' He hesitated and scratched his head.

'Yes?'

'Although, mind you, on occasions, when the subject of women came up especially, then he might freak and then, if he did that, you'd want to get out of his way fast, because then he'd well, then he'd go fucking mad.'

21

Jidney wrote to me after his conviction saying he had decided to send me what he enclosed as a result of our encounter the night I arrested him, remarking: 'I'm swiftanic, I am. I've always thought of myself as Mr Swiftanic, Mr Swiftie.'

'What?' I thought. 'Are you trying to be daring?'

I started reading in a mood of indifference because Jidney had been caught now and was out of the way, but when I had finished reading I corrected that judgment and sent it upstairs to the Voice.

Jidney refers to me as 'detective,' and leaves it at that. The heading is: 'Hell Opens Its Gates To The Public.' After pointing out that he has abandoned art in prison and taken to writing, because he is having to find a new way of talking about life, he starts:

'Well, good afternoon, ladies and gentlemen – here we are in the museum of hell. Even though it is only a museum, and neutralised, you might feel even so that it could come alive at any moment like a sleeping volcano – therefore it might be better not to linger too much over the exhibits.

'Here's a tableau – look at this woman's body. Her name was Mandy Cronin, as you can see from the label. She went in great pain; she appears to be trying to plunge through the floor like a listing boat. Here are her clothes that she took off in a corner, still warm, and look at her face in death – much smaller than you would think possible for a human being – turned to you as if it were still waiting for an answer. The answer, even if there were one, is stopped by the question in the mouth that fell half open in her last time; the congestion has turned the lips black.

'I am neat. A swiftie. I cut corners, live for power.

'I'm normal, sometimes for a long time – and then, I still don't know what happens quite, I get restless and shuffle the deck for a new game.

'Hell is a museum! The Chamber of Horrors is sterilised! The decayed evidence is arranged neatly, as exhibits in glass jars, with the blood, mess and putrefaction removed. I have nothing more to confess. In any case I am not confessing myself; I am acting as guide and curator to the museum.

'So I shall die in this prison, but I shall be back in a hundred or a thousand years; I've got my return ticket. Will anyone recognise me? Of course they will. I'm eternal. I may return as another outer "I", but the inner "I" will be the same; I never change. For the stone that was rejected by the builders shall be the keystone of the corner.

'Do you understand what I'm saying, Detective? Do you share my language? Does what makes sense to me make sense to you? I can tell you everything now, I have eternity in front of me. I now have time.

'I go here and there in my mind, pick dates at random; it doesn't matter.

'December 7th. Another most unsatisfactory year almost over – a new one ahead, perhaps the last. Everything is final now, irrevocable and flat, and I have started drinking again, which fuels my compulsion: I must continue with Ann, make a final effort to acquire and dominate. The complete understanding of another person. To penetrate the mystery of otherness – that is the art of my life.

'The money I spent on materials for my painting, on the video camera, lighting, sound equipment, various – well spent.

'Improve your mind. Everything interests me, therefore I have studied everything – the brain's determination to understand the brain. Art, mathematics, literature, cinema – I can discuss a wide variety of topics. That's how I hold women, through feeling myself the master of a conversation. Their submission makes me glow inside, whitening to the incandescence of final submission: *If London is incandescent, London is burning away.*

'Knowledge smooths the path to being unique; I discovered that in prison a long time ago. Being in solitary confinement and surviving it sets you apart; in the difficult block you can really explore the darkness. To know yourself to be beyond the reach of light – that reveals a terrible strength in a man, spurs him to extraordinary things.

'I feel old, inactive and full of foreboding – indeed today yet again it occurred to me to kill myself. It's part of the cycle. I have always said to myself, be cunning like a wild animal. But now, increasingly, my pleasure in being alone is turning against me. I am lonely and at bay; it seems that even a wild animal finishes as its own victim.

'Judith Parkes used to call me her "Mr Boastie" – but when I jumped her she screamed as she fled the world forever. As she screamed I drove my prick into her; it felt like fellating a fallow pig and then fucking it. My triumph and pride at getting her was so great that when I killed her it was a continuation of sex. What heaven! Stripping her naked as a savage, reducing her to gabbling fear and desire, was dark red poetry – you can't help creating divine poetry when the drive comes. Go for the loners, for the ugliest, like I did with the whore they called Dutch Gerda. She told me why she shaved her sex, so that she could still feel like a kid being fucked. Kid? She must have been fifty. That was years ago ... Of course, you get no view of what you might look like seen from outside by a third party, the experience crushes it out. Just as well.

'... And broke her neck. One moment I was leaning over her where she lay on the floor, her eyes discs of terror; the next, her neck tight inside the cord, one swift snap on my part and she relaxes, shrinks, falls in like a piecrust – not peaceful but still, not pale but waxen, unnatural, the sweat in her hair freezing.

'It seems odd when I think back, Flora being so religious. One day, after her death, I found a book of hers. She had pressed a flower in it together with a sheet of paper on which she had copied:

> Jerusalem, my happy home,
> When shall I come to thee?
> When shall my sorrows have an end,
> Thy joys when shall I see?

'Incredible, the things people find important – but then I know very few people, keeping myself to myself as I do. Paradoxically, I don't at all like my apartness from people being pointed out. I remember the night Judith said to me, *but we don't even know each other*, which sealed her fate. Judith was a schoolteacher; she exacted very high standards from people and had a great influence on me from the moment we exchanged glances on the bus, so that it was both insulting and exciting to be dismissed in her very severe tone as worthless, insignificant, a stranger. I subsequently taught her more about the meaning of severity than she would have thought possible, and yet here she is in the museum, look at her.

'Vary the pattern a little. Each victim suggests her own death to you – sometimes the knife, sometimes the wire, sometimes bare hands. You ignore the mess, wade through it. It is inevitable. It is the precise inquiry, the assault on the abstract.

'Evening birdsong outside; I forget the year. The people next door have put weed-killer down in the garden next door so that every plant has turned brown, bent over and died; I think they didn't read the instructions or forgot to dilute it. Christine has voided her bowels on the mattress behind me, so I let the blind down and turn her face to the wall where I can't see it. I was upset with her because she kept saying "It's hard to say goodbye, it's hard to say goodbye" each time I partly throttled her, till the din she was making got me down so much that in the end I finished her off before I meant to. Afterwards I was very depressed because it was another failure and I went and stared out of the window.

'How often have I stared blankly out of windows!

'I was in a dilemma over Ann M, aware of what I was going to do of course, yet I felt my dreams had faded and that there was no splendour left in me. I even had periods when I felt like letting Ann go. She was very frightened of me at times, but whenever I pretended I was going to finish with her she started crying – so here she is in the museum too, waiting like the others for the parts of her I left under the floor at Thoroughgood Road, people who in their way are still with me, and whom Ann will probably want to get to know.

'How strange it was to have all that money and never spend any, watching it grow in the Carat account. That makes me feel better for a while. Me, an orphanage boy! Rich!

'But I am depressed. Looking out of the window, how bleak it is – a naked garden in midwinter. My lack of excitement at everything I see tells me how far I have declined. This is one of the days I dread, when I wouldn't even care if I was caught, or killed. "Action" is the only cure.

'I don't know who I am today; I am going through wild swings of mood, veering from optimism to despair. This frightening but familiar disorientation is a bad sign for Ann; it means that the stranger who visits me is coming. During the period last year while I didn't troll I went to bed each night feeling: "That's another day I haven't hurt anybody, another week I haven't had anyone in my power."

'It was a great feeling, until memories of Flora stirred again; it's surprising how she still has the power to move me, urging me on now that I have met Ann. I like women like Ann, with very decided views – prim, strict and politically correct.

'We met at the Anguria; it was like dropping fat in acid.'

'Already, by the time I was seven, I'd start a day which I'd know was going to be different as soon as I woke up; I'd have funny ideas about what I was going to do with it which didn't come from me. The people in my head would be telling me to do such and such and I'd think up a cover story, and all the while I'd have my other, real story going, what I was really going to do. Only I'd know that what was planned would seem weird to other people, so that even though I'd know inside what this real project was, I'd just not be able to admit it even to myself, so I'd pretend it was just going down to the old bomb-site and skipping pebbles across the reservoir. Whereas the real idea would have been, say, setting fire to a hut out on the allotments, or else killing the neighbour's cat and then playing with it, getting ideas about it sexually and trying them out, that kind of thing. I was very precocious sexually; I was masturbating at the age of nine.

'At school I used to be very precise about the way I did things. I was always neat and very *physical*, anxious to prove things chemically – I'm still like that. I liked to handle objects, basically with the intention of altering them, changing their state, especially seeing what they would be like if they were dead. Sometimes the object would be an insect or a bird or a dog, and a lot of people didn't like that, wouldn't like the things I'd done to it. I didn't get on with the other kids. What they liked was fighting, football and girls. I hated girls. My mother made me be like a girl.

'The short time I was at school the headmaster used to send for me, and instead of beating me when I'd done something he didn't understand he'd start trying to explain things. He'd say: "Now, listen, what I want you to realise for your own and other people's sake is that everyone on the face of the earth is a *person* – that means that everyone's got his own skin, his own name and his own thoughts, do you see, which he's entitled to within reason, and every single one of these *persons* is *different*." He'd say: "You're the only boy in the years I've taught here that I've had to say this to – everybody but you takes it for granted."

'Only although I understood perfectly well what he meant, it was just words. I always listen very politely to people when they tell me things like that; I haven't the heart to tell them they're just a drone in the background and that as far as I'm concerned the speakers are exactly like the words, all alike. But I also know that isn't the right response, so I'm very polite – until the urges come over me, and then no one on earth means anything whatever, unless of course somebody's stupid enough to get in my way.

'There are more and more days now where I feel everything falling apart inside me. I get crumbling feelings, bits inside my head sliding about. Don't think this is recent; it isn't. I've always had it. Parts of my mind fly around in my head loose and I get dizzy spells, like a current switching on and off in there, till finally there's what feels like a short circuit, the ends of two wrong wires being put together; there's a shock with sparks and like a sharp cracking sound in my brain, and after that, whatever I do, it's nothing but a kaleidoscope.

'What's worrying is the feeling I've been suddenly disconnected. A period of time disappears; then events come together as though they had happened on top of each other, even though you know they can't have done. When you do find them side by side your brain feels like a compass needle going round and round on its card and then this needle suddenly reverses itself from north to south so that in the end you don't have any real idea what's going on. You know things are happening, that you're doing things; yet they just aren't real because they're nothing to do with what you're supposed to be doing, or it might be that you know perfectly well that you oughtn't to be doing what you are doing, it makes no difference. I have to appear outwardly as if nothing bizarre were happening, but that's just automatic pilot; it's like nightmares where you're autowalking into some place and you can't do anything to stop it. So the way I seem to be behaving at any given moment could be concealing something that I'm reliving from years ago. Not against my will. Because when I'm living through episodes like that I haven't any will. It's someone else's will; I don't know whose will it is.

'What I'm saying is that, during the periods when I am volcanic, in eruption, what is really happening is that I am present in past situations; I've just told you that once I've created a situation I have no further control over it. Events occur that are associated with other events that happened a long time ago, a past which is continually repeated and forms a pattern in itself; the result is that although I think I know who I am, and go on being that person, one day I meet someone new who triggers me, and then I'm confronted with what I call a certain *type* of situation. And then I find I have become another person with objectives altogether different from my own; it's as if the person I think I am had left the room.

'That old person, the absent one, is almost quite at rest. He is like a householder who welcomes a burglar, who simply hands over to him everything he has. He is shocked by the intrusion, of course, yet is curiously content to be replaced by this new person. So the stranger ousts the old occupant easily, giving him orders and achieving his wishes for him, enabling him to gratify all his secret and forbidden desires; all the old person has to do in return is to consent to being absent, a fragmented ghost somewhere on the outskirts of the new one for a while. The old person does not protest about this arrangement at all, has agreed to it, so that the new person is not in the least distracted by him. To the new person, for as long as he is present, the old person is nothing now really but a dead man upright.

'Only, when the old person has been allowed home again, back into himself to find the stranger gone, what has been done in the meantime, during his absence? He is left with what has been done by the new person, who is now a mere visitor dropping in from time to time to sample and savour the harvest of his actions. But what the new person perceived as an orgasm of pain and pleasure, the old person perceives as a scene of devastation – a dismembered, decapitated corpse, irrelevant, disgusting heaps, clumps of dirt, blood and matter scattered on a bare floor; in fact the results are seen by the old person, who was "dead" or "absent" while the action was occurring, to be as negative as the motives that prompted them, so that all the "old", or usual person inherits from the ongoing action is a horrible, bottomless sense of failure and futility, a blank despair where there should have been utter triumph.

'For what has been going on is the death of someone who has not only been subjected to terrible pain but also raped, and then forced to perform unwilled, unnatural and obscene actions against their deepest nature, and then, afterwards, even more urgently acted upon; meanwhile the old person has been watching, at first indifferently and unaroused (since he is uninvited, and so not officially present during the action) by the taking of life; the new person, the visitor, is taking care of that. But what both persons are thinking, of course, the whole time the new person is intent on his work and while the old person, though absent, is peering over his shoulder with a certain abstract feeling of pleasure, is that each in his way has affirmed and justified himself by virtue of their unusual mutual contract, that each is witnessing or performing the going into the general flesh of indifference, making an objective matter of proof, scientific and detached from revenge, of what can't be seized by the average man by singling out elements, particular red threads or pieces of human matter, isolating these physically and preserving them in tins, on film, or otherwise, in order to contemplate them in various ritual ways, thus working towards an eventual firm new order of universal togetherness.

'The new person, by temporarily banishing the presence of the old person, has fulfilled the wishes of both, through an act of destruction, by availing himself of the old person's loan of his strength and sexuality. But the new person was merely the executioner, a butcher hired for the event who, now that he has played his role, departs or else in turn stands aside so that the intricate activity, the psychic and intellectual processes of both persons, opposite yet complementary, can occur.

'I watch judges, psychiatrists and the like making their usual prolonged meal of the obvious. What is obvious is that I am myself a victim. People confuse what is compulsory with what is pleasant. To be obsessively locked into a single form of activity, as I am, is the hard, precise struggle of a scientist or painter. Like other masters, I take leave of my immensely difficult operations with the sensation that I have breathed history into the air – I abandon my work in a trance-like state, fulfilled, exhausted, as if I had created a masterpiece.

'Remorse? A priest who came the other day asked me if I felt any; I took one look at him and told him he had no

conception of God. I got them to take him away.
   '"The audience is over," I said, and burst out laughing.'

'History is an eternal newspaper; that is the definition of history. It is a linked series of stories, all of which appeared on page one of their times. What happened on the other pages is relegated to footnotes, or isn't mentioned at all.
   'By that definition, detective, I am without question a historical figure. I have appeared on page one. For someone seeking affirmation I have gone far; I have obliterated seventeen individual human psychic maps across whose frontiers I stride in memory as an undisputed tyrant and conqueror. Striking actions in life are the result of having refined life into what can be consecrated in a single gesture. To succeed, it is necessary to become a god and then, on achieving that status, to prevent the violation of the godhead by the criminal and irresponsible elements of society that surround us all.
   'People are so stupid to be disgusted at the pubic hairs I put in the tins, for instance, when all that meant was that I was at last near the meaning of love.
   'We are both beyond the condescension of the educated ignoramus, Detective – far removed from the simpering propositions of psychologists whose only true search is into the possibility of a university chair. These happy hypocrites have converted their patients' terror of the void into a six-figure income and a seven-bedroomed house. I knew that you understood all that by looking at you the night you arrested me; that is why I do not hate you and why I am writing to you. I am also told that you have enemies in the police. We are both alike to this extent – that, although our unease has different sources, when each of us sees his prey he corners and entices out its violence as a means of releasing his own; whether you arrest a killer, or I trick, rape and throttle a woman, we are each of us yielding to murderous instincts, as if the past which

humiliated us was still the present.

'I have forced time to offer itself up to me as a sacrifice with an ever-renewing supply of pascal lambs; as for the past, all I have ever wanted to do to it was slit its throat.'

'Hell is absolute, and as such unlivable. You are not meant to live in it; you have to be dead to live there. The only way out of hell is to become it; the only cure for the absolute is to become absolute, a god. But even then, when you are absolute, you are still not safe, for even when you have become a god you are still in a world that is not absolute, a world which has laws (the proposition, for instance, that all men are created equal) that no god can possibly recognise, laws that threaten him precisely because he has not made them – laws that forbid the making of the very sacrifices that are due to a god.

'I am whirled round on the fiery wheel of the impossible; I am in a dead end that just farts in the face of normal human life. Didn't you know that evil is banal? To fuck the same prostitute who wears the same grubby bra every night at the same price in the same room with the same damp wallpaper in the same corner, prick washed under the same cold tap with its irregular all-night drip, same screaming-match over the price for the second go, same spring squeaking as you turn over, same yawn, same snore, same police siren in the street below at the same time, the same pink neon flashing on the same square of blanket – why, if she's an idle pick-up it's easier to kill, abolishing the situation, having had nothing from it, and leave with your puritanical hand intact, the blood on it the proof that your image is intact. So I pass her the devil's kiss, the knife, and leave without paying, silently, my lips knotted with passion, purple, my knuckles contorted.

'Evil is dull and dangerous, like the army. It is for ever and ever; only its first fake beauty is seductive. I wore a hat at one time; my absurd idea, meant in all seriousness, was that my hat would cover my horns and I used to walk about the streets, thinking that.'

'What I have done, detective, is what we all most desire to do, each in his own way – to be beyond time, nature, people, years, women. I am a hero – and yet what's heroic about fighting your way out of a heap of shit?

'I slipped into a Soho club one night silently like a mad dog and stood alone and unseen in a corner listening to the piano there, watching the businessmen dance with night women in red who had stepped down from the microphone where they sang with the last of their voices, retrieving their old excitement, the time of pleasure before the time of doubts. But I could not join even their tired clan; I was apart; for no one, not even they, could tell me that what I had lived was just a dream, insubstantial; no one could put a hand on my shoulder and say: "Wake up – you never yielded to any murderous desire."'

'Relationships would undergo negative changes. Whichever woman it was, a time would come when I'd feel I'd got everything I could out of her alive; I'd get impatient with her as soon as that feeling started, until she irritated me each time she came into a room. I'd notice that I couldn't stand some little detail – her odour, perhaps, or her speech mannerisms; towards the end the mere sight of her would be like pouring petrol on an open wound. I'm really very aloof – an outwardly easy-going man on a short fuse. I'd describe myself as having a fixed standard of irritation with a low flashpoint. So once we'd get to that stage I'd want to speed matters up. I'd start drying up on an intellectual basis with her as well. You know, all her ideas that I'd thought fascinating to begin with – well, coming out of that same mouth now, hearing the same old rigmarole over and over again, it'd just make me want to start screaming – Flora offended very badly in that way

– and it would be the same in the sex department.

'One of the features that stays on in my mind about the Reg Christie case was the way Ethel stayed married to him all those years before he killed her at the end – it was his last murder and the one he knew he couldn't get away with. Even as a specialist I find it amazing that whatever she may have suspected about the deaths of the other women and the Evans baby she couldn't bring herself to believe that her Reg was involved; how could she have believed it of him, when she spent the last night of her life sleeping next to him in the same bed?

'Killers are like mushrooms; the deadly ones look like the ones you have for breakfast, unless you happen to have the sense to turn them over and look at the funny underneath.

'I think we might close the museum now, ladies and gentlemen, walk softly away from the barred door. I wake, and it's the night screw here on the maximum security block, slamming a door and double-locking it with a jangle of keys – a metallic noise like memory itself, the sound of his keys, not mine.'

22

After I had sent this material upstairs I heard nothing from the Voice for three or four days; then there was a 'phone call just as I came in from the scene of a shooting in a South London disco. The Voice said: 'You're going to take part in an exercise that I think you'll probably find interesting. I referred what you sent me from Jidney onwards, and it's been decided that the relevant police officers, under the guidance of a psychiatrist, are going to study Jidney's mentality for profiling purposes. Since you were the arresting officers, I have therefore nominated you and Stevenson to attend; Detective-Inspector Crowdie will sit in. Dr Argyle Jones will be the psychiatrist in charge; you'll be notified of the details in due course.'

He asked if there were any questions and then rang off before I had a chance to put them, the way he usually did.

'I don't know how they think they can take us off what we're doing,' said Stevenson, 'still, that's their look-out.'

'That's right,' I said, 'some poor bastard must be setting up the scream for more men the way we usually do.'

By the time I saw Jones I had had another letter from Jidney. I said: 'You'd better read it.'

The letter read: 'It's a bad day. I'm terribly depressed by this news that I'm to go in front of this psychiatrist. Why do they dredge me out of hell now, covered in my blood and slime? Why don't you just let me be? You'll never understand what it's like to be me. That's the only reason I write, because writing is the only way I can explain the truth.'

'He may think that what he's writing is the truth,' said Jones at this point, 'he probably does, but it's nearly all lies. He's totally self-obsessed – still, what else would you expect? He can't see himself from outside at all. He can't do what I call getting out of his car and walking round it. Wait till we examine him – you'll see what I mean.'

The letter continued: 'They say his name is Jones, and that he's a psychiatrist – I don't care what he is, he's never looked down at his hands and found blood on them; he's never lived in a flat world with flat people in it. I don't want to be bothered by questions of love and hate . . .'

'He does actually,' said Jones, 'he's dying for the treat, he's an exhibitionist, they all are.'

'. . . In fact I fall in love repeatedly. It's an obsession with me – only instead of blooming with love, I bloom as murder; it's called squaring the circle.'

'What a load of crap,' said Stevenson.

'Hell's full of that,' I said.

'Twenty years ago there was a whore at Borrowdale Road; I can't remember her name now, but you say she was the third. I had had my eye on her for a long time; we used the same pub over in Camden. I dreamed of killing her day and night for four months; I rehearsed it over and over. Finally we went back to her place; we got on fine till I did something to her in the night and she started screaming, and then when I came to I found I had raped her and hacked her to pieces the way I'd dreamed.

'Afterwards I looked down at her and felt very distant; I was sick and sweating with a great void inside me as if I were coming back from a faint. I remember thinking I couldn't go on like that; yet at the same time I knew it wasn't my decision. It's like when I used to wet the bed at the orphanage. I used to keep telling myself it wasn't me that had wet the bed, but it didn't help because it was always me in the bed. So to get away from the punishment I just went absent, until it wasn't me in the bed or anywhere else.

'Killing was the same. I cleaned up my approach; I copied people a lot for that; I'm a born mimic. After a disappearance I'd say to myself Christ, whoever can have done something sick like that, just like a normal person would; often it was a long time before I could accept it was me. That would be the early ones, as I say, where I only slowly realised that it was me who had taken these women's nipples off and placed them over their eyes and bitten into their stomachs and scrawled messages on their legs in blood while in the ritual trance.

'I killed to affirm myself and keep feelings of futility at bay; then often I repudiated the whole thing even while I was still clearing it up. I'd make sure I did it in a sensible place, I'm never random, I always got the person to the killing-place alive, by car usually. Once I'd got the vault going, of course, I did them all by car. But the first one I ever did by car I took to a condemned house – that was Brattiloe Mews, the piano-tuner woman I took up to Finsbury; that was the time I nearly got caught when some squatters broke in downstairs. Luckily they were drunk and I got rid of her under the floor without them hearing, and the next time I came by to see what had happened, to check if any police inquiry was going on, they'd bulldozed the house and cleared her away with the slurry.'

'He makes it all sound so simple, doesn't he?' Stevenson said.

The letter went on: 'I very nearly went to the doctor after her with these pains in my head. In fact I made an appointment, but at the last moment I was afraid it might lead to inquiries, so I dropped that idea.

'When I'm not trolling or courting I feel very disjointed inside myself; I'm aware there are things that don't add up.

The only time I add up is when I'm on the hunt, when I'm essentially not there, as I've tried to explain. I'm lucid afterwards, but by that time there's the blood and the bits and pieces lying about that don't seem to fit in – for instance, I remember looking at an arm on the floor with a cheap ring on one finger and thinking, what's that doing there?

'That blood-drenched floor at Brattiloe Mews still comes back to me sometimes. That, and of course the clearing up; I always remember that part because you have to think clearly and do everything in a very methodical way. Sometimes I get a feeling like vertigo, I'm tempted to leave clues, but then you take a pull on yourself and say sod that. Only the true crime books and the newspapers, most of them aren't interested in the killer's state of mind – they don't see any further than Woman Slain In House Of Horror, The Victim's Bedroom As Police Found It and all that.'

'He doesn't half ramble on,' I said, 'he's worse than a weather report.'

'What it is,' said the letter, 'it's God and Satan fighting it out. It's each other's throats they're after; it's their battle, and the best thing we can do is leave them to it. You don't want to know why they're in there together, do you? No. You lock the door on them and let them scrap.

'And that's all you know, Detective, and all you need to know – except one mid-afternoon I remember when I was young, there were the two of us coming away from the pub together, we had plenty of bottles, music on full in the pad, bare floorboards, wallpaper peeling off, no curtains to block off the street, the drink, the sudden wrong word, the swift rip of the bra coming off. My fury that I couldn't enter her, suddenly I'd got her down, then the unending moment when the tip of the knife's a millimetre your side of her grunting belly – irresponsible! The responsibility comes afterwards, if it can find you. But by then it's done, and what you get as a pay-off is cheap relief – it's good and evil that bank the real profits of her slithering about in her blood. Then later you're aware of the gore all over your dick and you look down quite waggish and tell it *you was well out of order there, son*, and then when the blood's dried on you go and lie down on the bed and pick the little crusts off.

'People never really go into the killer's state of mind. They only think they do – I reckon it's because they're too frightened of what they might find buried in themselves if they really got in there. Frightened they couldn't get out again. So they do it the easy way, waste their time trying to assess a killer by their own standards, it's just childish, you can't catch the moon in a butterfly net. They're up against interchangeable man, the gregarious loner, the man with another man to go with him who's got to be disguised as a normal man, because he's not that abnormal that he wants to get caught. All those old prats you see at a safe distance on the box putting the moral point of view about murder, priests and so on, they ought to spend a night with me alone in a room. There'd be no violence – old men and bores don't turn me on – but we could have a talk, and they'd be singing a very different tune in the morning.

'People ought to see a serial killer when he's in between times – he's as safe as a parked car! You could drink a pint with him, you could share a room with him!

'A killer wouldn't mind being normal – he's a hyena that would rather be just a man in an armchair, and he can give a good imitation of one, too. If he's living with others he does his share of the housework and washing-up. Nine days out of ten he's just someone walking up to the off-licence for beer and cigarettes – people can't seem to get it through their heads that even if a man's a killer he's still got to find a place to live, pay the rent, get a job, buy clothes, go out and get pissed; he feels up, he feels down the same as a normal john. When he feels good he gets up, gets dressed and goes out; when he doesn't he just sits in his sunny room, contemplating the quiet dust of hell.'

'Do you believe that bit?' I asked Jones.

'Yes,' he said, 'as a matter of fact I do. No one can be in the state of turmoil necessary to kill twenty-four hours a day.'

'The bad part for me,' the letter continued, 'is that when I kill I take all my pleasure at once and then I've nothing left for afters. I can't take things slowly when I'm active. Using a camera to get the pleasure back doesn't really work either, any more than the keepsakes do. Often I watch the films and I think, sod it, I might as well be watching Mickey Mouse. Even admiring the left-overs in the tins doesn't really work; dead body-parts aren't interested in fighting back. The dead don't care any more what you do, so you wind up feeling frustrated, like someone's standing there watching you with their hands in their pockets laughing, while you're just going through the motions. What's even worse, you know that any minute the fantasy'll be over and then there'll be nothing left to do but go through the whole thing again.'

'He's making a better job of himself now,' said Jones.

'He's certainly graphic,' said Stevenson. 'I've read plenty of killers' writing, but I've never heard anything as clear as that.'

'That's just what makes him so interesting for our purposes,' Jones said. 'When we've finished the whole lot will go onto a computer; it'll be analysed, filed and added to all the rest of what we've got. Mind, he's not typical. Very few of them go on killing into old age like that.'

'There was Fish,' said Crowdie

'Yes,' said the psychiatrist. 'Yes, there was Albert Hamilton Fish.'

'People always try to put themselves in the place of the killer,' the letter went on. 'It's a waste of time, they never get it right because they have to try and deduce it. They imagine that because they see killing as a nightmare, the killer thinks it's a nightmare, too; he doesn't, of course. Killing's an explosion like any other, and when it's over you just feel sad and empty, and there's nothing to be done but wait till next time, till you can say, *Go on, son, get up to the West End, go trolling the bars, make your opportunity like everyone else.*

'You never think any differently. You feel bad sometimes – but then who doesn't feel bad about some of the things he does sometimes? That's not going to make a scrap of difference, or anyway not for long – feeling bad never does. Even when you're sitting on a bus or in the pub or going up to pay the gas bill your mind's always going to be running on women, it's a pattern; the only difference is that sometimes your hatred of women is loaded, sometimes it isn't, it's a mood – we all get moods. But when you do feel put down, or remember how you've been manipulated by a woman, taken advantage of, especially when you've been drinking, then you feel yourself being loaded. It's exhilarating, that is; it's like being a gun and feeling a clip of ammunition going into your butt; you're a weapon come alive. The woman you pick doesn't have to be the one that insulted you – with me it's my mother, so it couldn't be, she's dead; but it might be someone who reminds you of her, that helps.

'Although in extreme cases where you've got to act, pretty well any woman who turns up might have to do, depending on the urge – but usually you can choose, and that means you're making progress, emerging, beginning to show your power, growing up.'

'There's a bit more at the end on the last page,' I said to Jones, 'but none of the end part's really very interesting.'

23

Before going over to the prison to see Jidney, the four of us met in Poland Street in room 202, which was Stevenson's office.

'I don't want Jidney to hear this in front of you,' said Dr Jones. 'On the other hand, I think it's advisable that you hear it, it's bound to come up.' He rummaged in his briefcase and found an audio cassette. 'This was with the rest of Jidney's belongings at Thoroughgood Road,' he explained. He went over to the tape recorder while the rest of us found ourselves chairs. He said: 'This was how Daphne Hayhoe died.'

The tape was Jidney talking to himself.

'I told you right away why you had to go, Daphne. It's for the same reason that the others had to, so that I can have you to myself without any impurities; once it's over there cannot possibly be any unexpected disappointments. Then, all being well, I'll be able to make this great painting of you that we discussed. You may be right in arguing that part of me doesn't understand what it's doing, Daphne – what you really mean is that the part of me that wants you to be like me is dead. But it's got to the point where I would only find you increasingly dull if you went on living, so that we shall have to have each other the only way we can.'

'Christ,' I said.

'I remember the other night, at the same time as we had

that discussion, we discussed one or two practical details regarding Carat Investments, after which I told you I couldn't wait any more. "We've talked long enough now," I said, "we've discussed everything important."

'Whereupon you said you knew there was no escape.

'Do you remember that, Daphne? You really surprised me when you said that. One minute you were saying you loved me, that you understood, having made your will, left me the houses, opened Carat Investments for me and repeated you wanted to die rather than leave me and because of your parents' suicide – and now the next thing I suddenly get is this rubbish about there being no escape.

'You said that you would have talked to me about it further if we had had time, but that if I couldn't control myself and hold back any longer, well then you could see I had no choice. I remember every single word of that. I told you I didn't mean to use excessive force, but even so you said: "I shall still die, Ronald, and now, at the last moment, I'm not sure I want to. Isn't there any other way?"

'Well of course there wasn't, Daphne.'

'The bastard's proud of himself!' Stevenson shouted.

'I tried to explain the ritual aspect to you one last time. I remember your face clearly while I was talking to you, and I remember every word I said. "Imagine you are like me and that you have these waves of beauty beating over you," I said, "spread out over a period of several months; finally they lead up to the climax that you and I are going to have now. If you were an artist – a poet, for instance, or a composer – you would understand right away that what I am talking about is creativity. When I get the urge to create – and I can feel it coming on weeks, months beforehand – I get up one morning and go out all over the city, meet people and draw inspiration from them. Then, having made my choice, I invite my new star home and get to know her, weaving her into an interior ritual of my own, developing an approach to her in exactly the same way an artist develops a feeling for his model."

'I said to you: "When I conceive, Daphne, which I often do, it's always in an empty bed. I lie on my back gazing at the stark ceiling, waiting to be fertilised in bare rooms. Darkness is best – places with drawn blinds, neutral and absent with the smell of dust. My experience of women, of beauty, is too intense to be experienced directly; I have to dissect and absorb, and for me to be able to do that properly means that beauty has to be calm. For what is the definition of art? Art, Daphne, is the removal from beauty of every element that is random or unnecessary. To be eternal, beauty must be captured motionless. Nothing irritates me more than that refuge of the second-rate, for instance, the cinema. All those stupid people running about – Dürer or Van Gogh would have had a fit! No: any irresponsible, irrational movement is alien to beauty and detracts from it. The gravity of beauty is its quietness. Beauty is what life was the instant before you caught it. Beauty is a graven figure arrested in a moment of fire. Eternity never dies, Daphne; it remains in the mind forever, enabling the artist to express his act of love."'

Stevenson and I listened in a state as close to disbelief as we would probably ever get.

'You said: "But I shall turn to dust, Ronald."

'"Please understand, Daphne," I said, "you were never much more important than dust even when you were alive; you were a vision in my mind."'

'How does he manage to talk about her in the past when she's still there in front of him?' said Crowdie.

'You understood and said: "I have made my peace, Ronald."

'Our last moments were sad. It was death in slow motion, explained step by step; it was the first time I had explored this avenue so thoroughly, and the extraordinary restraint I had to exercise increased my pleasure enormously. I got her to undress and lie down on the floor, naked, whereupon I tied her up. Then a remarkable thing happened. As she was not in her first youth her singing voice was not very good, being cracked, and hoarse with fear, too, naturally, but as I came over to her with strangling wire and a great hard-on, she closed her eyes with wrinkled lids and sang out firmly:

> Christians, with a gladsome mind,
> Praise the Lord for He is kind,
> And His mercies shall endure,
> Ever faithful, ever sure.'

The tape crawled off into silence. 'It reads like a boring catalogue,' said Cruddie, 'until you realise it's all true.'

'You can't expect a very boring man to make his life sound interesting,' said Dr Jones.

24

The following are extracts from the notes of Dr Argyle Jones, made during a series of interviews with the accused:

> 'My body's growing old, and I can't mend it,
> My life is leaving me, but I can't end it.'

Jidney claims he wrote these lines after the death of Judith Parkes during a period of depression – typical of the moods that he claims he endures after each episode, when he says he 'shrieks in his darkness to be delivered'.

Background: Jidney educated himself chiefly in jail. He is proud of his good looks, which his mother either ridiculed by forcing him to dress as a girl, or else denied in some other way; she was a child-beater and a child-hater. While serving previous sentences he gained a reputation both with staff and other prisoners for his painting and studies in art, in which he received a degree from the Open University – he also took elocution lessons from a public school detainee which have left him with an almost neutral accent. He expressed what he felt about his achievements in an early interview as follows: 'I gradually came to feel that by expanding my interests I had acquired a new control over myself, and that the justification for everything I did had become clear. I could abandon various puerile habits, compulsive masturbation, for example, and rationalise my attitude to women through direct confrontation. I was now evolving in a self-affirmative situation.'

I asked him to elaborate on why he feared women to the extent that he felt compelled to kill them.

Jidney: 'There is no question of my ever having been afraid of women.'

(From Dr Jones's notes): Jidney is a peculiar-looking, as well as a peculiar-sounding man. Jarring elements are evident which he managed to suppress while at liberty, but which strike the onlooker forcibly now. His speaking voice is out of character with his face, which relapses into savagery when he gets carried away and forgets that I am looking at him, particularly when he is recounting his childhood and youth; whereas when we are discussing his crimes he is almost always objective and offhand in a tone as expressionless as his eyes.

He usually appears to stare through, not at me; when I return this look he remarks: 'Oh, I see what's got you excited – the famous flat look of the psychopath! But I can make my eyes dance, I can make them sparkle – watch.' He then puts on an animated, expressive look, accompanying it with a smile which he manifestly takes to be natural. I believe he really thinks he has convinced me that his act is real. He says: 'I see you are looking at my smile now. If you'd known the battle I had to be allowed a steel mirror in my cell; I could never have learned that smile without it.' But he is incapable of any truly spontaneous gesture at all; everything he does or says is studied. All the same, he is very sensitive to my reactions to him; he carefully monitors every response I make.

Overall, he reacts in the way I would expect of a patient whose intelligence has replaced his personality which, for as long as there is no trigger to activate it, is absent or asleep, dead.

We went into the day's interview.

Jidney: 'No one will ever know me. The view of me that

others have in inaposite – what useful judgment can onlookers pass on me when they have never known my brand of love?'

Jones: 'Can you describe that love?'

Jidney: 'It involves the destruction of everything capable of love – of women in my case. Love equals manipulation. The death of one woman stands for the destruction of all women. If love equals punishment, then I exist to prove that hatred can punish also. The woman has the same symbolism here as that of the pascal lamb.'

Jones: 'That is one of your preferred images.'

Jidney: 'Yes, God is risen, but he has got out of bed in dark clothes.'

Jones: 'Do you feel now that your actions, these crimes that you have committed, were wrong?'

Jidney: 'Is it wrong to want to have a crap? What do you mean, wrong?'

Jones: 'I meant objectively wrong.'

Jidney: 'I can only be objective about situations. I can't be objective about women. Applied to women, it depends if I am there. I don't know what you mean by objectivity in this case.'

Jones: 'Yet you have claimed to have feelings of remorse.'

Jidney: 'You must have misunderstood. All I experience are feelings of extreme disappointment, feelings that it will go better next time.'

Jones: 'And has it ever?'

Jidney: 'No. Each time it's simply a body, an object on a floor or lying in a chair. It has also become a liability, something that has to be moved. It is just an object like a table. All I have that lives are memories – of one person or another passing from life into death. Nothing else. I stop vibrating when the woman stops vibrating. Apart from the memories, apart from what is irreversibly over, I feel I have been blindly singled out.'

Jones: 'Singled out by whom?'

Jidney: 'By no one. By my drive to affirm. It's always the same. I am a lone instrument of punishment, with recourse to no one.'

Jones: 'Is that a primarily sexual drive?'

Jidney: 'The sexual part of it is symbolic of majesty.'

Jones: 'You are being most articulate.'

Jidney: 'I have educated myself.'

Jones: 'Turning to another aspect, you had no hesitation in profiting financially from your victims.'

Jidney: 'Of course not. At school the master used to say: "Industry is what makes the wheels turn." Gain is logical.'

Jones: 'And that was uppermost in your mind when you got Daphne Hayhoe to set up Carat Investments for you? After you had persuaded her and at least one other of your victims to make a will in your favour?'

Jidney: 'Everyone has to live. I know what poverty means. I grew up in it. The vision that "most people" have of the world is non-dimensional; they have no conception of depth, richness, colour, no idea of the elaborate ritual of pain and terror. The depression after the event is a small price to pay for self-fulfilment. I like to drink and talk to the victim for weeks, months, all night and all day. In some cases – with Daphne Hayhoe, for example – even the victim became fascinated with her destiny. As for hatred, it is co-equal with love; I experienced that with my mother. Before she became an alcoholic, which happened around the time I was born, neighbours told me she was a strict churchgoer, a member of the Lewisham Sisterhood Of Faith and yet, morally upright though she was, she could not leave her fanny alone as she forced me to witness. She also had to punish me for having witnessed it, but gradually I persuaded myself that I was disembodied so as to reduce the pain.'

Jones: 'What factors influenced your choice of victim?'

Jidney: 'Only women who were very prudish about sex really counted.'

Jones: 'Were you generous with them? Financially, I mean. You had plenty of money. For instance, were you ever generous to Flora?'

Jidney: 'I wish I could have just bought a nice coat as a surprise for my Flora.'

Crowdie: 'Flora is dead.'

Jones (to Jidney): 'That is not what I asked you.'

Jidney: 'Flatter and spoil those who are about to die, pay them all the attentions of a lover – that's only right – give them everything they want except the one thing they can't have, myself, because it isn't there.'

Jones: 'Will you please try to answer the question.'

Jidney: 'Well, no. I wouldn't say generous. You see, as for money, I have always lived in a very quiet way. I was a businessman. Property.'

Jones: 'So you are implying that you were mean with money.'

Jidney: 'I want to be quite clear about this – Flora told me I had a most engaging personality, a kind word for everyone, a natural charm that many people couldn't resist. The people who do resist me treat me as a joke because I have no sense of humour, of how I look from the outside. I despise such people; they are of no interest to me at all. They are not victim quality. I know my victims at once; the first glance exchanged, and there is the sacrificial message.'

Jones: 'Were you ever aware that you were putting on an act with your victims?'

Jidney: 'Not necessarily aware, no. Of course I am a natural actor. If I had had the training I should doubtless have been a great actor. I have a sense of ritual. The void, the black depression, the violence – that surfaces only on close acquaintance, but by then of course it's too late. Until I have the victim in my power she must never see me as I am. So I suppose that, yes, I am an actor.'

Jones: 'Tell me what were you thinking about last night.'

Jidney: 'Last night I was looking at my penis. It was limp, flaccid; I was thinking it couldn't be the same one that ejaculated as I struck, hard as an iron bar and pumping, pumping in an orgasm so total that it revealed and exalted me to the core of my being.'

25

Jidney: 'I want you to read this.'

Jones (reading): 'The only honesty in men is their recognition of the purpose they know to be in them and which a few of them refine and narrow down until it emerges fully. This can only happen once the seeker after control has learned to create the necessary situation and face the challenge. Mine is a nihilist purpose, so that honesty means the extent to which I express my disgust and hatred of the world; as in every sphere of self-affirmation and fulfilment this expression must be either ultimate, or nothing.'

Jones: 'What do you feel about death? Is that nothing?'

Jidney: 'Yes. To a nihilist, everything is nothing.'

Jones: 'But you get a feeling of achievement from nothing.'

Jidney: 'Yes. To procure a death requires planning, determination and courage.'

Jones: 'I am referring to your own death.'

Jidney: 'I never think about my own death. Perhaps I die with the others in some degree. I don't know, I have never thought about that.'

Jones: 'Please go on.'

Jidney: 'To put someone to death requires energy and *drive*; you would be quite wrong to assume that killing is a simple matter. The hero, the lone commando running towards an enemy with a bomb, do you think that's a simple matter? Yet what both I and the commando experience is the same challenge. Both are driven towards a seemingly impossible objective; mine is the mastery of hell.'

Jones: 'You are getting excited.'

Jidney: 'It is exciting. People become so used to their everyday selves that their interior behaviour, until it is criticised from outside, seems natural to them whatever it is. Man is aware that he transcends himself only at supreme moments – moments in which he is carrying out actions that he knew he was born to execute, and I suppose the difference between myself and others is that the others never plan for a supreme moment.'

Jones: 'I would like to hear more about that.'

Jidney: 'Yes, I have a statement to make there – no experience can acquire any dimension unless it is absolute. Therefore it is meaningless to ask me whether I was aware of the nature of what I was doing while I was killing; the question is absurd. Not only was I aware of it, I was supremely aware of it; in fact I was aware of it from a height so great that my awareness amounted to absence. Nor is it any use your asking me whether I think that what I did was wrong. I don't think in terms of right or wrong. I think only of the inevitable. I act only in response to the irresistible. I do not make solemnly-graded judgments about life or death with pursed lips; what is the point, when everybody knows that both are irreversible and inevitable? That is why I confessed willingly when I was caught, and have never complained about my capture; it was the sacrifice exacted by triumph. If my sentence were to be death, even a painful one, I should accept it without a shrug; I have no argument with the inevitable. I accept what has in any case always been a part of me; I even welcome it, just as my victims did. That is my view on capital punishment. My life is irrelevant; what matters is that I should remain alive for as long as my doing so is a means of continually asserting my power.

'This is where the serial killer differs from murderers of any other type, and it explains why I describe myself, not as a monster as you do, but in the way I saw my victims, and as I see myself – a negative martyr. As for remorse, which you spoke of before, I know what remorse is supposed to mean, but I have no idea what it is. It is outside my terms of the absolute; if I cannot experience a feeling absolutely, then I cannot experience it at all.'

Jones: 'Have you any further comment you would like to make about feeling remorse, or not feeling it?'

Jidney: 'Yes, I think I have said, the nearest I can get to remorse is perhaps sometimes missing someone whom I caused to disappear. But what some observers – prison visitors, would-be penal reformers and some killers, too, who parody it simply to help an interrogator prove his own theories in return for easier living conditions – what they take to be remorse is in fact no more than the occasional lucid period, moments of terror when the killer temporarily realises the gulf that separates him from other men. But this mood is no more than the normal result of any catharsis – a feeling of bemusement and emptiness, of anticlimax after long drawn-out preparation, of the struggle against the yielding to desire (which increases it), the result of the physical infliction of death itself.'

Jones: 'Does the fact that the general public hold you in abhorrence make any impression on you?'

Jidney: 'Certainly not. I am not immune from natural enemies – nobody is – and my own adversaries are those whose role is to procure justice for the weak, such as these other gentlemen here, and those who share their views. But for the man who exists only for the supreme moment the weak have no meaning – nothing besides that moment has any meaning. The killer is a primitive, which is why he is hunted and brought down. But I would also point out that he instinctively knows his pursuers' tactics – and that is why I have existed amongst you undetected for so long.'

Jones: 'You are proud of yourself then, of your instinct, your prowess, your stature.'

Jidney: 'Of course I am. I am a very affirmative person. By the way, I should like to add a remark concerning some quite wrong opinions I have heard regarding killers of my type. Firstly, they are not stupid. I myself am of above average intelligence; I am certainly capable of appreciating the difference between profit and loss and of running a business, as you know. Secondly, they are political. I would assert that there is no such thing as a socialist killer because, short of death, concepts such as equality, let alone liberty or fraternity, do not exist for the believer in the inevitable. Therefore every serial killer is a fascist. In other words, fascism is not a belief; it is a course of action natural to the wild beast, rooted in primitive nature, which the killer too not only accepts but welcomes.'

Jones (to us): 'Who was that Frenchman who wrote "*tous les criminels sont des jésuites?*"'

26

We were at lunch, and Stevenson had been reading Dr Jones' notes. 'What does he mean here by the aura phase?' he said to me. 'Christ, you need a whole new dictionary here.'

'It means he's living in a dream world. Don't worry, I had to ask Jones too.'

'Of course he's living in a dream world,' said Stevenson, 'and that's why seventeen dead women tell us how dangerous the bastard is.' He passed Jones' sheets back to me. 'As for his mind, it feels more like looking inside Christie's kitchen cupboard to me. Do you really take all this sitting and listening to him seriously?'

'You bet I do,' I said, 'it's science summing up instincts that you and I have had for years. And at last it's official – we're going to give psychological profiling a chance. Don't you see what Jones' interviews with Jidney are for? It's so that in a few years' time we'll have files on convicted serial killers that spot common factors in all of them right across the board, so that in the end we'll be able to nail them almost as soon as they get off the ground. We're a long way off still, but at least we've stopped being childish, we're finally admitting that we're ready to learn – but we are still learners, we can't afford to give ourselves airs. But once we've learned the rules I'll bet we'll be good at it. With a bit of luck it'll tell us how many madmen there are running about the country convinced they're the fucking prince of darkness and killing the way we light a cigarette – and maybe by decoding and entering their world we'll stop any more wretched women being butchered.'

'You're coming on like some kind of radar,' Stevenson said.

'That's right,' I said, 'new tricks for the street. It evens up the odds a little, and I heard Cruddie saying you're on the next course too, so you'd better get reading.'

'Buy you a pint first.'

'Why not?' I said, 'I reckon we've earned it. Why don't we go up to The Sicilian Defence – judging by this case you seem to get all sorts in there.'

'It's quite a paradox, really,' Jidney told Dr Jones the same afternoon. 'The less normal you are, the more normal you have to be.'

I told Jidney that nine bodies, including those of Flora and Daphne Hayhoe, had been found so far, either in the vault or buried in other graves near it, most of them with their genitals missing.

'You've some way further to go yet,' said Jidney, giving me an arch look. I thought it was one of the most frightful expressions I had ever seen on a face.

I managed to keep calm. 'Ann Meredith,' I said. 'Why don't you tell us about her last hours on earth?'

So he started telling us – quite easily, calmly, as if he'd been to see an average movie the night before and was giving us the plot line. Ann hadn't understood right away, he said; when she did, he described her face, whiter than a wall when the shock penetrated, wobbling and weaving in the middle of the floor, her knees caving in under her.

'What?' she had asked him. 'When?'

'I told her what I told most of them,' said Jidney, 'that it depended on her really. But I remember I added as I often do, *Why not now?*' He pulled out his prick in front of her, which was her first sight of it, seized her by the back of her neck ('got her by the love-curls') and forced her head down on it.

'I want you to eat me now,' he said, repeating it to us the same way through his teeth as he must have said it to her. 'Make me come, and then I'll make up my mind whether to keep you alive or not. The more pleasure you give me, the better your chances.'

'I can't, I can't,' said Jidney, mimicking her voice, and I don't know how I didn't get up and hit him. He broke off to tell us: 'I don't think she believed I was going to let her live, she was too bright.' He went on: 'So I told her, *you've got ten minutes to be the goddess of love.*' Suddenly he was beside himself. His eyes, which were always flat, lit up suddenly like the rest of his face, triumphant; he was right back in it, plunging through that moment. 'Come on, I told her, do it. If you make my big man here droop, you die, so let's have less talk and more action, your tongue's got other work. Fucking women. Enjoy it, and make me enjoy it – I'm big enough, aren't I? Hey, aren't I big?'

Later, in a different mood, he said: 'If I could remember what I'd done, of course, it might have been different. I might never have been able to do it.'

'But you managed it all right,' said Cruddie.

'All right, well, as you proved I did it then I must have done it.' He added after a moment, 'I have to admit it's amazing how much of my behaviour seems to have escaped my observation.'

At lunch in the prison officers' canteen Jones asked me: 'Are you finding any of this of value?'

I said we all were.

'Don't think I'm just scientifically pulling the wings off flies,' said Jones, digging into his tinned steak and kidney pudding with gusto, 'I have long wanted every suitable officer to understand the application of psychiatry to police work by watching it in action.'

27

'Let's talk about Judith Parkes,' I said to Jidney. 'Do you remember what happened to her? Do you know where she is now?'

'She's where I can always find her, in a quiet corner, where we can talk. It's in a flowery place, an old church out in the country. But I haven't been down there for years.'

'Perhaps you've forgotten the map reference,' Stevenson said.

Jidney said: 'She must have changed a good deal by now.'

'I think she got tired of waiting for you and left,' I said. 'I think she's in the morgue.'

He looked confused. 'Oh no,' he said. 'She'll always be where we parted, I made sure of that.'

In the afternoon Jones started on a different tack. 'I want to talk to you about your mother again.'

Jidney : 'You mean before Boy moved in?'

Jones: 'Yes.'

Jidney: 'My mother – Ida we always called her, I don't know why, her real name was Gertrude. She would say when she caught me killing things, "I'm going to punish you for your own good," and then she'd hold my hand over the gas jet on the cooker. Afterwards she and Boy screwed and made me play games with them while I'd be thinking, I'll give you two such a shock one day.'

Jones: 'And your father?'

Jidney: 'I never knew him. She kicked him out of the house before I could walk. Later on the neighbours told me she used to beat the shit out of him when he drank. Anyway, one day she just shrugged and told me he was dead. She was a very religious woman in public, very sharp in her speech. She never went out with Boy in public. He used to come round to the back at night, or stay in the outdoor privy all day till it got dark. Reconciling the way she behaved to the neighbours, and then what she did indoors, and my skirts, hand in the gas flame – that caused a lot of problems – the bedroom stuff with her and Boy and then, in the street, butter wouldn't melt in her mouth. I always had troubles there, when you could talk about what went on indoors, when you couldn't; it was always hard fitting what the three of us did to what she told the neighbours – things to be talked about, things not to be talked about. If I came out with anything I shouldn't, that was my skin flayed off when we got in. After she died I got talking to one of the neighbours and found out she was never known as Ida or Gertrude in the street – always as Mrs Jidney. Always.'

Jones: 'So you always had to be on your best behaviour.'

Jidney: 'That's right, but she punished me anyway if she felt like it. That gave me a completely different face. Inside I was nothing like my face. I was the opposite of my face. I can behave well for a long while, it pays to behave well in jail. That's where I learned to behave for years so that I could earn time off a sentence, so I worked out this system where I stored up what I called enough credits for being no bother until the day when I'd got enough credits and could lower the barriers and let rip, let the built-up pressure go bang like that and didn't have to be no bother any more. I'm not nice, I hate being nice, I just pretend to be nice, and then I reward myself by doing what I really want.'

Jones: 'Do the words good and evil really mean anything to you?'

Jidney: 'That's not what you're talking about, is it? What you mean is, did I just run about like a maniac slaughtering women, not caring one way or the other, or did I work the odds out so as not to get caught? What we're really talking about is being caught, isn't it? Well of course I didn't want to get caught – look around you in here, terrific, isn't it? – but my problem there always was that I could never be sure what other people were going to find odd about me. It meant I had to be a good actor. It's exhausting, though, trying to insure against everything, it's like backing every horse in a race. Pulling the bet off time after time starts as a challenge but it gets harder as time goes on. I had to think my way into being normal, I had to say to myself: "As long as I think I'm normal I am normal." I'm like a bomb, sometimes I'm unarmed, inert; there are times when I can get drunk, be alone with a woman, nothing funny's going to happen . . . But if I get in a certain situation and there's a trigger there, then things do happen, I get into overdrive, and then it all happens so fast. Even though people say that it physically takes the victim a long time to die, to me it doesn't seem long at all.'

Jones: 'One question I've been wanting to ask you. Can you think of any historical figure that you feel you identify with?'

Jidney: 'It's interesting you should ask me that; that's a good question. I always wanted to find out how evil I was by getting to know about other really evil people, people in history. Once I got into my teens I started reading everything I could find about murder in the press and in paperback books. But I couldn't really find what I wanted; all these murderers had only got themselves written about because they'd been caught. The exception was Jack the Ripper, but he hadn't really killed that many women, only five, and then he'd bottled out. My revelation came at the end of the war in '45, when I was fifteen and still at the orphanage. One of the masters at school said I behaved like Heydrich, so the others called me Jackboot Jidney, and it stuck, so I thought I'd try and find out a bit about this individual.

'I didn't know much about Reinhard Heydrich at first, except that he was a sadist who played the violin – like I get pleasure from art – was number two under Himmler in Hitler's secret police, was promoted to governor of Bohemia at thirty-eight, and that murder was meat and poultry to him. Straight away I identified with Heydrich; straight away the kick I got from him was his urge to power.

'I started going down to the clothes markets looking for the kind of gear he wore in his photographs. I had his picture stuck up all over the place; once I had a few bob I even had gear made so that I could dress up like him, and when I was doing my first stretch in the nick I had books about him sent in. He wasn't a lifetime thing with me – one day a couple of years later I threw everything about him away; I was out on my own by then and didn't need him any more.

'But while he was with me it was powerful. As a murderer he never went wrong – how could he? He had a licence for it. And it never bothered me that he was assassinated – you can't assassinate a god. I had him with me, inside me, beside me, all the time; I think that accounted for the intellectual look women say I have – Reinhard was very intellectual-looking. First-rate mind, secretive, a plotter, relentless, a cruel bastard, great fencer – Olympic standard, but mind you didn't beat him, he hated that – dancer, musician, womaniser, liked a drink, long, slender, feminine hands. Evil? Court-martialled and cashiered from the navy for rape, history of sexual abuse of women, got his rocks off with flagellation, hiring prostitutes for heavy punishment after an evening playing Beethoven sonatas in somebody's drawing-room.

'And forgiveness. Forgiveness was something special that I brought in; I don't think Reinhard ever considered pardoning his victims. Posthumous rehabilitation was my own contribution to mass killing – after all, magnanimity is the quality that marks a god off from a mortal, and a god who can't forgive the insults paid him by his victim – well he isn't a god at all.

'People mistake my laughter. It's disguised laughter. It's the laughter you expect to hear at a happy party, in an atmosphere of jokes. It's nothing of the kind. I can't use the real tone of my laughter because it would reveal me. The real tone of my laughter is the sign that I have designated the woman I am laughing with as a woman I'm going to kill.

'Just before I'm going to kill it turns brown inside my head and there's a charred smell in my nose like burnt paper.' He turned to Jones and said: 'By the way, it's something I've been meaning to ask – what's the point of our talking like this exactly? What's the purpose behind it?'

Jones: 'Part of my work is to establish whether you're aware that an action has an effect and, if so, whether you are aware of the nature of the effect.'

Jidney: 'What you're implying is that you're sane, on the grounds you've never killed anyone, and I'm not.'

Jones: 'That's definitely relevant, yes.'

Jidney: 'Then that should be the end of the matter.'

Jones: 'It isn't.'

Jidney: 'I'm not going to insult myself by saying I'm mad; I'm more like an obscure branch of mathematics. Even just talking to you now I'm thinking as a double negative. It's a paradox. I talk to people the same way that it seems to me they talk to each other, only I overdo it each time I want to prove I exist. It's an upward spiral. The more I have to prove that I'm like them, the more I demonstrate that I'm not, until it turns out I've no option but to kill someone so as to prove what everyone should have realised in the first place. The world won't accept me as a part of itself, so I do conjuring tricks.'

Crowdie: 'That's a new word for murder. Conjuring tricks. I like it.'

Jones: 'It's a question of whether you can analyse your motives for the conjuring tricks, of whether you've any insight into them.'

Jidney: 'I'm feeling very lucid today, so I'll try to explain. If I had the insight, there wouldn't be the tricks. The tricks are instead of the insight. Don't forget about the old person and the new person, the writing I sent this detective here. Don't forget about what I call the visitor. The man you're talking to now, he's not the visitor, he's the householder; he's the man the visitor comes to see. The visitor's got no insight, only desires.'

Jones: 'Negative desires.'

Jidney: 'If half of a man'd been punished from birth for the sole reason that he was born, you might say punished out of existence, that half had to go somewhere, it didn't just disappear. Supposing that instead of sitting there with a pen it was you that had drawn a life sentence at birth and were sitting in a cell for doing something you couldn't even remember – being born – something you hadn't even done? Wouldn't something happen to you? Supposing you didn't top yourself, wouldn't you sit up thinking it was you and say: "I've got to do something?" Yes probably you would, only you'd find that whatever you did, you'd be doing it out of compulsion; you'd find that whatever you did would turn out to be wrong. Because the only fantasy you would have would be a negative fantasy and you'd behave just like me, completely upside down – you'd go out and kill so as to belong.'

Jones: 'Knowing that's wrong?'

Jidney: 'What killer ever knew anything right? Remember also that the man who brings death is never surprised by it. He's familiar with death the way you're familiar with the woman you married, and what I've just been trying to explain to you is why, to me, love and death are the same.'

Jones: 'But your victims were human beings.'

Jidney: 'Human beings haven't earned my thanks. If you're me you know nothing about human beings; you can only guess at them. I wish you understood what it was like not to be a human being, to be beyond human beings, to be a thousand feet above the world on a tightrope, watching human beings stare up at me, all their faces the same because of the height. Come on, doctor, try some vertigo; don't spare yourself the nightmare. But you don't understand – I think only clowns and acrobats understand, because there's a link between circuses and murder. The world enjoys gawping as long as the risk's only the price of a ticket; the audience wouldn't think it was much like entertainment if it were up there itself.'

Jones: 'You feel no guilt.'

Jidney: 'How could I? The visitor doesn't fancy having sex with women. What he fancies about women is killing them; it's like wanting a beer and getting the cap off the bottle – thirst makes you an expert all over.' He shook his head, laughing. 'Does it mean a man's in a fugue when he's going down to the pub, does it mean he's sick in his mind when the only image he's got in his head is a bloody pint?'

Jones: 'It does if he's an alcoholic. What we have to understand about obsessions is that they're only superficially like pleasure. No one who suffers from an obsession enjoys it, and the point of existence is to enjoy it as much as you can.'

Jidney: 'Listen, I just act, I keep telling you. I act fast. Swiftanic. I don't feel guilty. If I feel guilty the visitor comes by, otherwise, if I had the insight, I'd feel guilty the whole time. But no one can do that; he'd fall apart. Take bedwetting.'

Jones: 'Yes, you often talk about that.'

Jidney: 'I wet my bed right up to when I was thirteen, right up to when I started doing the other things. Sure I felt guilty. I felt guilty because I got punished. On the other hand, what was the use of feeling guilty about something you did the whole time? I wasn't going to suffer non-stop just because I was guilty; there were other things in life, such as paying back. So I got in the habit of doing whatever it was, and then not thinking or worrying about it – that left room for the visitor. That way I adjusted to what I did the same as everyone adjusts.'

Jones: 'Last time we were talking about your fantasies. How do you feel about those now?'

Jidney: 'The difference between my fantasies and yours is that you fantasise about what you *like* to do or better still about what you are *going* to do; whereas I have fantasies about what I *have* done; I relive in my mind what I *have* done. I learned from being punished at the orphanage that what I found natural other people regarded as abnormal. But I'd decided it wasn't; I decided that I made the rules for me.'

Jones: 'Tell me about setting fires. How old were you when you set the first one?'

Jidney: 'I was ten when I set the first one; it was an old hut in some allotments.'

Jones: 'Why did you do it?'

Jidney: 'Because I needed to; you don't do things you don't need to do. First, it was like the animals – setting fires was destruction, it was getting my own back. Also, the fires fuelled my fantasies. I hated women because of the way my mother hit me when I wet the bed and for smashing things in the house. She nearly killed me twice; the worst time, I had to go to hospital.'

Jones: 'What was the matter with you?'

Jidney: 'She always hit me on the head, and not with her hand, mind. I had to go because she hit me with a broom-handle, the second time she threw a hot iron at me; I got it in the face.'

Jones: 'What happened when you got interested in women sexually?'

Jidney: 'I wanted to fuck them, of course, only the wrong way – I mean really screw them – nails, hammers, whips, throttle them, torture them with ropes.'

Jones: 'You must have realised that wasn't normal.'

Jidney: 'I don't think I realised much at all. Talking of wrong, everything in my life was wrong, so I daydreamed it was my version of all right.'

Jones: 'Daydreams? How do you feel about those now?'

Jidney: 'They've dried up. There's no more splendour, no sun on the mountain.'

Jones: 'Does that depress you?'

Jidney: 'It's worse than that.'

Jones: Could you explain that further?'

Jidney: 'It's a feeling of failure. I've let myself down. I thought I was special, a one-off, an original. But now I don't think I was so original after all. Listen. One of the people I killed was called Mandy Cronin. I used to be back at my place masturbating, and I'd have fantasies about her the whole time. You remember, we talked about her before, she was one of the early ones I took down to the vault. When I got her down there I remember I said to her: "I've got to kill you now, right away, I can't wait. Now this breast here, now the thighs, now the buttocks, that's it, let's get you spread right apart." I did it to her a thousand, ten thousand times before I did it. But what I don't like remembering was the last thing she said. She said: "Wherever I'm going, I pity you, Ronald. I pity you because you've got no margin. You think you're demonic but you're not, you're nothing, you're pathetic, your killing me isn't going to prove anything." Now that hurt. That offended me in my pride, what she said there and I killed her straight away, but she'd already spoiled the whole thing; it was all spoiled because of what she'd said.'

Jones: 'What do you think she meant when she said you had no margin?'

Jidney: 'I think she was telling me I was the opposite of what I knew I had to be; she was telling me that I'd just got a little mind.'

28

While he was relaxing in an armchair before the first hypnosis session began Jidney said: 'It's different now, when you're questioning me about it, of course, but when I actually went out to kill it was just a terrific feeling of anticipation I had – you know, like going to meet some alluring female stranger you'd only spoken to on the phone; you knew it was leading up to that moment when you were going to be face to face with the person you knew you would kill. There was a sweetness in the atmosphere between you when you would first meet the person and you'd want to prolong that, spin it out over weeks and months – probably it was the nearest I could ever get to falling in love. I don't know what it was that made the hatred in me feel like love; all I know is that right up to the period when I couldn't wait any longer and took their lives they brought me the end of loneliness.'

When he had hypnotised him Jones said to us: 'I think a good deal's going to come out. Ronald, can you hear me now?'

Jidney: 'I'm sleepy but I know I'm talking. I can't stop talking, it's terrible. I'm dizzy, I'm falling down. I mustn't do that. When I fall, I get confused.'

Jones: 'I'm leading you out of the confusion, Ronald, I'm taking you by the hand. It's quiet here, there's only the two of us, no one else can hear. It's like vomiting, you'll feel better when you've got it up. I'll help you. Go on, Ronald, do it, vomit, take all the time you need.'

At this point Jidney was violently sick.

Jones: 'There's plenty of time. Take your time, recover, we can wait.'

Jidney: 'What are you waiting for?'

Jones: 'For you to remember about behaviour.'

Jidney: 'You mean this behaviour now?'

Jones: 'No, not now, your behaviour at the time.'

Jidney: 'What time? Do you mean with Judith?'

Jones: 'If you like. Or with Judith, Ann, Daphne, or with Flora or Mandy if you like.'

Jidney: 'Well I remember them all! What's so special about Judith that makes you single her out?'

Jones: 'It was you who singled her out.'

Jidney: 'It was behaviour like any other behaviour. I don't know what you're driving at.'

Jones: 'You're lying, Ronald.'

Jidney: 'I have to, otherwise it would mean I'd have to start noticing.'

Jones: 'That's what I want you to do. I want you to trust me, Ronald, I'm your friend. I want you to suspend judgment, let your guard down.'

Jidney: 'You're asking me to start caring? A machine? I can't do that. It's breaking rules.'

Jones: 'You and I both know we have to break rules. It's the rules that are stopping you getting better.'

Jidney: 'You're flouting power.'

Jones: 'Don't feel flouted, Ronald. I've taken you into this quiet place, you and me together, we're in this garden. No one can hear us. We're friends. We're here to learn from each other.'

Jidney: 'I'll try to get to it slowly. Say I was the onlooker at my own despair. I'm sitting high up in a box – it's a theatre. I'm nothing to do with what's going on, but I lean forward and suddenly I'm down there under the lights. I don't know what to do or what to say, but I've got to speak and move if I want the power.'

Jones: 'More power than most people?'

Jidney: 'Most people don't know themselves; that's why they haven't any power. Or else they don't need it. But I've got to have it.'

Jones: 'Supposing you didn't have it? Then what would happen?'

Jidney: 'I'd be nothing.'

Jones: 'Nothing at all?'

Jidney: 'Nothing.'

Jones: 'All right, but you have got the power.'

Jidney: 'Yes, now I've got the power, each truth is a portion of flesh to be enjoyed; each rule is a bone to be broken. Gnawed. I'm like a starving man. But you mustn't cough over what you enjoy. You mustn't choke on it.'

Jones: 'It's hunger.'

Jidney: 'It's the hunger to be.'

Jones: 'Food.'

Jidney: 'What's the matter with you? I don't feed any the less heartily because I talk to my food while I eat it. The more you need food the more intelligently you should treat it, except that you can't have intelligent food. No. That's not right, I haven't put that right. What I mean is, you can't have your food running about screaming on the plate – it's logic that you have to kill it first. Then you can talk to it. But it's obvious you have to be cut off from your food so that you can cut it up. You want something – but you can't have it screaming, that'd be like your power refusing you.'

Jones: 'That sounds mad to me, Ronald.'

Jidney: 'I don't notice that.'

Jones: 'And when you're not hungry what do you do? What do you do between fits of hunger?'

Jidney: 'I don't know, think about nothing much, sit in the park, have a lager, trace kingdoms in the dust.'

Jones: 'Do you feel different from other people?'
Jidney: 'I don't know. I'm no one except when I'm in power. When I'm not in power I sleep – I dream to pass the time. When I wake, when I'm in power, it's nothing but a single jump to murder – not the time a sigh takes to ask for pity, not the length of a scream.'
Jones: 'What about the other person's right to live?'
Jidney: 'Right? What do you mean exactly? I'd like to know more about what's behind that remark.'
Jones: 'I'm asking if you ever respect other people.'
Jidney: 'Power isn't based on respect. Still, the answer's simple enough – I can't live unless I can match my hunger to my greed. So let's suppose it was you I'd picked for my victim. I'll tell you what we'll do – we'll multiply my pain by yours, multiply it by two or twelve or twelve hundred or twelve thousand; I'll unpack the Sony, set it up and we'll film the whole movie, the full tragedy, the trusting flesh really sprayed out, the meal splayed out in rotten corners, mottled with horror.'
Jones: 'Earlier you told me that you once let a meal go.'
Jidney: 'That was Christine. Have I already told you about her? Did I tell you how I was coming to her and she looked me straight in the eyes and said: "If you're so strong, why do you always take life, never save it?" I turned away from her, shrunken. That's when I learned that power could never destroy power.'
Jones: 'Tell me what made Christine so powerful.'
Jidney: 'I realised that she wanted the whole answer and that she wasn't frightened of it.'
Jones: 'Weren't you afraid she would betray you if you let her go?'
Jidney: 'I knew she would never betray me, and she never did – if she's dead by now, it's not through me. I told her, I've got nowhere to go, so you'll have to come with me, and she said, *But I'm luckier than you, I have got somewhere to go, there's a door here right in front of me*, and she just

walked through it; I never saw her again. She caused the one after her that I took later the same night to suffer more, that's all – I said as I went into the second one *Well, if I can't beat life, I'll at least make sure it can't answer back.*'

Jidney was silent for several minutes; Jones let him be.

Jones: 'You've been quiet for a while now, Ronald, but I don't want you to stop talking yet, so I'm going to take your hand again and lead you out of the silence. It's calm here under this tree, it's in bloom, come and see, it's sunny, look at the clouds, can't you smell flowers on the wind?'

Jidney: 'No. We'll go out again and have another wreck. Since death's so final let's have plenty of it. Life's difficult? Let's make it impossible! I chose each of you in your dark corner where you'd been waiting for me for years – Ann! Daphne! Judith! Flora! Wait, all of you! I can hear you fluttering, trapped in the sitting-room corner, little grey wings, little birds! I put my hand into the cage – I can smell the first one, Gerda, that old prostitute I knocked off when I was just a kid! You all knew I'd come, and I had the courage to come for you, and now here I am. A quick twist, the pleasure – don't forget how grateful you all were to me. Gratitude? What thanks do I get? Are you laughing at me?'

Jones: 'Nobody's laughing.'

Jidney: 'Somebody is, I can hear it. You could kill me with that, I can't stand it, it's like a stake through the heart.'

Jones: 'I'm going to wake you now, Ronald. You won't remember what you've been saying when you wake up, do you understand?'

Jidney: 'Yes.'

Jones: 'I shall count to ten. You won't remember anything.'

Jidney: 'That's right. I won't remember. I won't understand anything. I know nothing. I am nothing.'

29

Next day Stevenson, myself, Crowdie and Dr Jones were sitting with Jidney again at the prison. Dr Jones had said to us beforehand: 'The psychotic has very definite aims.'

Now, when Jidney had joined us, Jones said: 'You have a very real purpose in being mad.'

Jidney: 'Yes. The purpose is to put increasing pressure on meaning.'

Jones: 'Yet the desire to be invisible is itself impossible and therefore mad.'

'Perhaps,' said Jidney, 'but even so, the overriding idea is to force the god out of its corner, to make it explain, compel it to appear, to account for itself. The intensity of focus on the objective and desire for it is in direct ratio to its attainability – the more unrealisable the objective, the more overwhelming the need to grasp it – despair in the knowledge that it is unattainable being so deep that it is blotted out – indeed, the sufferer's entire personality is blotted out.' He turned to a warder who, incredibly, was studying for the church in his spare time and said: 'I am here, therefore God is obliged to love me. If God is in all of us, then I must make others helpless, because that is the only way I can make the god in them listen to me – they'll never do it as free agents, of their own accord.' He turned away from us and added: 'I look out of this window, and everything outside, the sky, the trees out there, is bright, empty. Life is so bleak, I can't tell you how bleak.'

Later the same day, while we were having a break for tea, he remarked out of the blue: 'It's quite real. I feel it coming – death comes in and we stand looking down together at what I have done and say to each other: "Yes, what we have done here is quite real."'

Later, Jones took us aside and said, out of Jidney's hearing: 'Let's recapitulate. Jidney's terror is so great that he has been cemented into it – the rest is bravado, the shallow front of horror. But of course his fear must express itself, and it does so in the form of his distorted, nightmare recital, the grotesque re-enactment of injuries to himself and others. Let us divide Jidney into Self 1 and Self 2. Self 1 is not really aware of his actions, even though he knows he is present – Self 1 mustn't, and therefore can't, be aware of them, because the whole point of the entire Jidney's attempting the impossible is that Self 2 should bear the entire responsibility for what Self 1 knows perfectly well is wrong. But Self 2 enables Self 1 to disclaim all knowledge of right and wrong. The entire *raison d'être* of Self 2, the reason for his creation, is that he should in turn visit the terror on a third person (the victim), an action of which Self 1 is completely unaware, thus discharging it from the consciousness of Self 1, who has always been and must always remain innocent. The function of Self 2 is to shield Self 1 from all terror, absolve him of all responsibility, all guilt, all knowledge, even. But, because both selves know that this joint operation is an impossible one, neither can ever be satisfied with the result so that, just as in the case of certain mythological judgments – Sisyphus, for example – it has to be repeated for ever.

'So, you see, what we have in front of us is a man engaged in a nightmare attempt to banish his own shadow – indeed, the well-worn phrase "being frightened of your own shadow" takes on a new meaning.'

★

The next morning Jidney met us again in the room that had been set aside for us in the prison and told us that he had had a dream about God. 'God took me by the sleeve and said: "Do you see all those people killing each other?" "What?" I said. "Do you mean they can really feel all that pain? Who's responsible?" "I am," said God. "I never told man that I didn't exist. I'm on everybody's side, which means that I could never have existed." "It sounds to me as if you had been invented," I said to God. "There is great power in invention," God answered, "you should know."

'I have always had these conversations,' Jidney added, 'sometimes with God, sometimes with absent or dead people. Some of them I know, the others introduce themselves. I hear them as clearly as I hear you –' he pointed to his head '– in here.'

Going on to talk about his art, he explained to us that he was the new evangelist.

'The challenge in art,' he said, 'is to be continually on the edge of truth without ever going over it.'

He insisted that any sportsman, murderer or artist would tell you the same, and that he himself existed in all three.

The following is from some notes that were taken of what Jidney said the same afternoon:

'What is a revolution? It is a situation in which the judges are put on trial, overturned by popular mood. The parental promise has been broken, the nurse has failed the patient, the doctor has gone on an indefinite holiday when in fact the fever was at its height and the people has woken to find itself as abandoned as I was, the sheets filthy, the blanket stolen, the ward empty. So it took the blind, instinctive measures of despair.

'I am a paradigm of all that is desperate in society. All its illnesses are to be found in my illness; not to interpret me correctly is to interpret nothing correctly. Not to interpret what is alienated in society is not to interpret the causes of the facts lying on the floor with their skirt over their head and a knife through them. The purpose of language and art itself is to tell us . . .'

Jidney was taken ill at that point and we had to break off there.

30

'Before he arrives,' said Dr Jones, as we waited for Jidney's warders to usher him back into the room, 'I should like to give you the benefit of an idea I'm developing for a conference later on in the year.' He took some papers out of his briefcase. 'Let us see if we can make an appreciation of Jidney from another angle, based on what we have learned about him so far.'

We waited.

'Since we have recovered several samples of Jidney's artistic work, it might be instructive to compare his work to the work of a great painter who recently died and to see whether, and if so to what extent, it is possible to equate the artist's view of society with the assassin's. Accordingly I have taken a recent assessment of the painter's work (I apologise to the author for adapting it) and have replaced the painter as the subject for discussion with Jidney, thus placing Jidney at the easel – or, if you prefer, causing the painter to commit a murder in the place of a work of art. I shall now read this to the group, and I think you will agree with me that the curious and not uninteresting result is tinged with frightening overtones of the absurd, which I hope to use as a basis for further study.'

He gazed at us across the top of his spectacles but, as we did not react, he merely said: 'Here goes, then' and began:

'It seems to me, first, that we risk a tendency to overvaluate Jidney, to get him out of proportion – to raise the stakes too high, or drive them in too deep. He enjoys the reputation at the moment, as he goes to trial, of being the most celebrated mass killer in the country. This has nothing to do with his being at the forefront of murder, it seems to me. Except at the very outset of his career Jidney has been out of step with the motions of contemporary murder. No, his particular fame rests partly on our placing him as the last outpost, or possibly the last gasp, of the great assassinating tradition in sexually-linked murder – it rests on our placing him alongside killers with the status of, say, de Rais, the Ripper, Christie and, more contemporaneously, of Nilsen and Bundy, Gacy and Dahmer. And it is partly to do with seeing Jidney as the assassin of our time, to do with the almost musical pleasure that he derived from gaining financially from his victims – from the psychotic experience of the killings themselves (raised, in his own mind, and on his own admission, to virtually symphonic proportions) – that he is upgraded to the position he now enjoys.

'Hs stands as a murderer who provides pre-eminently a portrait of his age. It corresponds perfectly to one of the age's self-images – its conviction that it knows more about horrors than any previous age. Jidney's career has satisfied that criterion, even confirmed it. Speaking to colleagues who have examined him, he has seemed to several of them to represent what amounts to a heroic act, yet another proof of our capacity to face and outface the worst. But this is a light from which he should be retrieved. To see Jidney's work as an unmitigatedly appalled and appalling statement of the condition of modern man and woman is misleading, for Jidney's work can also be seen as the psychotic version of comic art, and this is not paradoxical – horror and comedy are often allied.

'Looking at three of his earlier murders, as in the course

of examination he has provided us with asides on them, it could be observed that it was only what could be termed the sincerity of his disgust, expressed in the savagery of his actions, that saved them from what would otherwise be mere *grand guignol*. But why assume that unless Jidney is truly, madly, deeply disgusted, unless he is transmitting a sensation of pure torment, then he must be some kind of phoney, an accused man trying to find a gap between medical knowledge and retribution in order to avoid punishment? That is to ask for an opus without internal drama and without overt performance. One could hardly apply such strictures to Ronald Jidney. Jidney is, frankly, a flesh-creeper. His life has been devoted to making flesh creep, slip, seep, burst, smear, crawl and leave a trail of blood. But he has accomplished this with terrific sweep and flair and verve. In spite of his talk yesterday of working directly from and upon the nervous system, his work is no stranger to display. Blood perhaps, but with gusto.

'You will remember that we were all present when one of my colleagues, in what was intended to be a devastating rebuke, compared Jidney's activities to Walt Disney's. He noted "the surprising formal similarities of their work." And it is an observation that sticks, in my mind at least. Consider the typical Jidney scene, as typified by the video recording in the vault – the body writhing as he sexually assaults it on the existential bedsit stage. Everything that is not flesh, everything that his method will not take to – clothes, furniture, other props – is visualised in a bold and bright notation. And even the bodies themselves, acting out the bouncy lines that their torment lends them, are like cartoons, only violently mixed-up ones. What makes Jidney's damaged bodies so particularly alarming, in fact, is that they are cartoon personages whose conventional invulnerability has suddenly been broken through. Yet, at the same time, the victim retains in her appearance something of the cartoon's ability to "bounce back". To explode, in cartoon terms, is not a catastrophe: it is its *métier*. This fact limits Jidney's ability to record the actual catastrophes that he causes – hence his apparent objectivity, insouciance even (except under hypnosis) when describing them. Even when he was describing the murder of his own mother, which happened in front of him, there was little he could do in language to distinguish this cardinal death from the inevitable disaster areas into which he converted every human figure.

'We must never forget, of course, the horrible difference between the artist and the psychotic – the first works of course from the model, the second immediately from the flesh; painting was never, and could never have been enough for Jidney; you do not have to be knowledgeable in art to realise that Jidney, whatever his aspirations, had little or no talent for the canvas. Having said that, however, Jidney was very much a performer, his work a visual display of his perpetual, internal making, unmaking and remaking. He speaks often of "vulgarity" as the element to be avoided, to be destroyed by subjecting it to various "controlled accidents" – introducing the "irrational" and then "taking advantage of whatever happens next". He has an enormous, one might say an irrepressible gift for reducing a lively, fleshly surface to chaos, and the caricaturist's knack of extracting a likeness from chaos. It was this illustrational impulse that required the flesh of his victim to disperse; it then recouped these pieces into what seems to us disturbingly ungraspable swerves of flesh, half optical blur, half physical slurp.

'Risk was of course at the heart of Jidney's work. There was the risk that the accident might prove unusable. There was also the risk that the attempt at an image would coalesce into mere proficiency. In certain scenarii a delicate balance was maintained between the image and the virtuoso formal invention. But the despised "vulgarity" was always lurking there, sustaining the effects, and sometimes peeping through a little too much – suggesting that if the distorting operation was suspended entirely, only a glib facility would emerge. In his later work, it can be seen that those ungraspable ectoplasmic manifestations settled down into something straighter. Jidney describes faces (in the Flora Borthwick case, for example, and that of Ann Meredith) as appearing in slick and often cute solidity – the flesh only marginally smeared; he recalls observing what would, in his earlier period (which, after all, spanned thirty years) have been once-evanescent highlights determining themselves in his memory as a blob on the end of a nose. As we have all seen in his last work, the Meredith case, the body had become a twisted and amputated cartoon, a Disney nightmare. Jidney's hand and "vulgar skill", as he refers to it himself, were then on show too clearly.

'Jidney should not be over-revered on his insane pedestal. He is a brutal murderer, not the great worker in human suffering and mortality that he would like to be described as being – indeed, often believes that he is. Leaving aside, if that were possible, the abominable terror, suffering and death that he has caused, his effects (even, with hindsight, to himself) were very much surface effects, with only a very transient ability to satisfy him – if you like, one aspect of his madness was his unwearying pursuit of the impossible, his sad, obsessional drive to recreate the experience until it did permanently satisfy him.'

'My purpose in this inquiry through substitution of one career for another, that of a painter of violence with a violent man, gentlemen, has not been to equate the artist with the assassin, but merely to attempt to argue whether, and to what extent, a comparison between the two states is possible, and, if so, where, to what extent, and why.'

We made what we hoped were appropriate noises and shuffled our feet; Stevenson lit a cigarette.

★

On the last day, after he had finished with Jidney, Jones asked the three of us out to lunch, because we weren't due back on normal duty till the morning. Sitting at a quiet table in the upstairs restaurant of the French pub Jones said: 'Well, all I have to do now is to compile my report – that, and Jidney's whole case file, will go onto the Yard's new computer, when it's ready, and from now on every serial killer we catch will be analysed in the same way, and this information will be available to any police force which finds itself with a case of this type on its hands.'

He took a sheet of paper out of his pocket and spread it out on the table, pushing the plates and glasses aside. 'During the whole of my examination, the criteria I have had to satisfy are the following twenty-one questions, which were elaborated by the Behavioural Science Unit of the FBI under the name of its initials, VICAP, and form the psychiatric profile of any serial killer. A positive answer to two thirds of these questions or over means that the public has an individual in its midst who is guaranteed to give you three gentlemen a headache. While I am reading them out, think back over Jidney's statements to us during my examination of him, and decide his positive score on the following for yourselves. Has Jidney exhibited signs of:

1. Ritualistic behaviour.
2. Masks of sanity.
3. Compulsivity.
4. Searching for help.
5. Severe memory disorders and a chronic inability to tell the truth.
6. Suicidal tendencies.
7. A history of serious assault.
8. Deviate sexual behaviour and hypersexuality.
9. Head injuries or injuries incurred at birth.
10. A history of chronic drug or alcohol abuse.

11. Alcoholic or drug-abusing parents.
12. Having been a victim of physical or emotional abuse or of cruel parenting.
13. Being the result of an unwanted pregnancy.
14. Having been the product of a difficult gestation period for the mother.
15. Interrupted bliss or no childhood bliss.
16. Extraordinary cruelty to animals.
17. Tendencies to arson without obvious homicidal interest.
18. Symptoms of neurological impairment.
19. Evidence of genetic disorders.
20. Biochemical symptoms.
21. Feelings of powerlessness or inadequacy.

When he had finished reading he removed his glasses. He gestured at the questionnaire, looked at the three of us and said: 'I hope you've all learned something. At last, thank God, we are all going to work together, not in spite of each other; it's official policy, and we are all going much further into all of this.'

31

The morning Jidney killed himself I met Stevenson as he was coming out of the cell; he had to slam the door hard to shut it because that was the only way it would close. He said: 'That's the end of Jidney. Amen.'

'Did he leave any word?'

'A note to say it wasn't what you've done that matters but what you've realised. He said he'd spent his life in the wake of people who cast shadows hoping to learn how to throw one. That he had visited death on people as his only means of knowing it. That it obliterates without being unkind. Those were the only things he said he had learned.'

I saw the departed man in Stevenson's face. He looked like smoke, a grey substance.

'What did you think of the note?'

Stevenson said: 'Can you conceive of such a thing on paper as a grateful scream?'

'I don't know what you mean.'

'You do,' said Stevenson, 'only you don't remember it. It sounds like the noise you made when you were born.'

We left. I had no answer for Stevenson. Like everybody else, all I could do was keep going, sometimes away from misery and greed, but more often, for reasons that you needed only to look around you to see, towards it.

It was vital to go on catching people like Jidney, vital to

play out the game against evil right to the last card.

All at once I am speeding after Dahlia, who is wobbling down our front path on her bike. Next week, she'll be nine. I am rushing after her with my arms open and calling out: 'I love you! I love you!'

But she is always just out of reach.